CAMPO

Debra Iles

DEDICATION

With love and appreciation to the Common Scribblers,
Alex Baker, Susan Larkin, Julie Wood

Chapter 1 – Kevin Conley, CAMPO

Kevin Conley was twisted around the writing surface of a chrome classroom chair, battling his charcoal and paper. In the second week of night school figure drawing class, his sketch looked warped and stiff. He couldn't relax; he couldn't get the left elbow right. Tonight, Kevin was not in the zone.

An aging man slouched naked on a green velvet stool in the center of the classroom, circled by twenty students. Caucasian, probably 5'10" and 190 pounds. The man gazed upward at a da Vinci drawing tacked over the classroom clock. His right elbow rested on his knee; his fist supported his chin. The man sighed and shifted that left elbow by two inches. Kevin set down his charcoal, closed his eyes and laced his fingers together, inverting them in front of his chest for a deep stretch. He took a slow breath, cracking his neck first at the man and then at his drawing. He picked up the charcoal again.

He was already thinking about break time, twenty minutes away. Struggling to refocus, Kevin stared hard at the old man's right foot and started to rough out the shape, wondering about the man's life journey and what had brought him to figure modeling in his twilight years. Curiosity softened his grip on the charcoal, and the lines began to smooth.

It had taken Kevin three years to gather the courage to take figure drawing. Shortly after he joined the campus police force—referred to by everyone as

1

CAMPO—Kevin had enrolled in a studio art class after work. At first, he told himself it was a healthy alternative to killing time at the local watering holes or in his too-quiet apartment, but gradually he copped to the truth that he had rekindled an ancient love. He had been the quiet kid who doodled; he could still conjure up the special energy in the art room in high school, the rustling of papers and earthy scent of clay and brushes bristling with inspiration.

Following his late father's path to the police academy, Kevin steeled himself to put aside childish pursuits. His goal was to join the city force and work his way up the ladder. CAMPO was initially a steppingstone toward becoming a big city detective—maybe even the Chief of Police someday. But after taking those first two art classes at the university, he had realized that his employee benefits enabled him, if he kept it up, to earn a master's degree in fine art. That fantasy took root, and he imagined joining the procession on a warm spring day, wearing the traditional cap and gown of a scholar and newly minted alumnus. He decided to stay with CAMPO a bit longer. That was six years ago, and now at the age of thirty-five, Kevin was happily on the cusp of earning that elusive degree.

His time on campus wasn't really a hardship. There was a bright energy to the young population, and he had learned to enjoy the seasonal ebb and flow of the academic calendar. Kevin was surprised that he didn't find the work boring; it was always something different. Chief Mulally often reminded the team that the university was the size of a small city, with the whole array of saints and sinners that any city would shelter. Kevin had been promoted to detective after only three years, something that never would have happened on the city force. Granted, the job was not all glamorous. Because it was a small force, everybody took their lumps on the more tedious details that appeased visiting parents, politically active students, and student newspaper editors. They strove to be both visible and discreet at football games, freshman move-in day, and concerts on the wide lawns. Sometimes it felt like they were play-acting law enforcement; other times, things could get very, very real.

Over time, Kevin had also become accustomed to the rigid social hierarchies that governed campus life. The faculty was at the top, then the students, then all the others who made the institution function. Jobs that required uniforms, like his, were at the bottom. On the plus side, Kevin had found that the campus force attracted the more thoughtful types on the criminal justice spectrum. The real knuckleheads and the power-hungry ego cases couldn't handle what seemed to them an upside-down hierarchy.

His mind still adrift, he chewed his knuckle and checked the clock again. Thinking about work brought his mind to the new case that had cropped up yesterday: an art theft, something he hadn't seen before.

Mid-afternoon at CAMPO headquarters, Chief Mulally had called Kevin over and assigned him to investigate a break-in on the West Campus, at an empty dorm room in Waverly Hall.

"That seems pretty routine. Does it need a detective?" Kevin had asked, resisting the urge to roll his eyes.

Mulally's glare told him to button his lips and get going. Mulally always bristled at the hint of insubordination, but he was more like a grumpy dad than a hard-ass boss. Kevin pulled a final draw of cold coffee from the mug on his desk and grabbed his spiral-topped notepad. "On my way, Chief," he said. He grinned as he turned to go. Mulally hated being called chief.

It was a ten-minute walk to West Campus and the September day was unseasonably gusty, so Kevin zipped his jacket up tight and hoofed it, trying not to notice the gale that bit through his pants. He distracted himself with a favorite pursuit: envisioning the best vantage points from which to capture the elegant symmetry of the quadrangle's Georgian architecture and towering oaks.

At most of the dormitories, the superintendents worked out of basement offices, reached by a steep set of exterior steps on the backsides of the buildings. Kevin found the green sign labeled "Building Office" and walked down the stairs, pushing the door open as a bell tinkled to announce his arrival. It was a standard-issue office with white cinderblock walls and high casement windows. Kevin looked beyond a pallet of toilet paper and a few open cartons of cleaning supplies to the seventies-era metal desk where the superintendent was just setting down her People magazine. Heavyset and graying, she wore the standard issue goldenrod hoodie with the university crest, unzipped over an identical polo shirt, loose at the collar. At a glance, Kevin pegged her for a lifer and guessed she would have a voice wracked by a million cigarettes. She introduced herself and the voice didn't disappoint.

"I'm Dory Johnson. It's about time you guys showed up."

"Detective Kevin Conley. Good to meet you. Can you show me the apartment?"

She stood and gestured for him to follow. They headed back outside, then around to the front of the building. As they walked, she answered his routine questions with an impatient tone, as if she were putting higher priority projects on hold for him.

"When was the break-in?" he asked.

"It wasn't technically a break-in, seeing as how there was no forced entry," she replied.

They reached the door to apartment 12C, at the end of the hall on the first floor. Dory made a show of finding the right key on the clattering ring she pulled from a chain on her belt loop. Opening the door, she waved for Kevin to go in first. The room looked like a still life from twenty years ago, fully furnished with heavy drapes and a

Persian carpet covering the parquet; there was even a faceted liquor decanter with glasses on a mirrored tray table in the corner. This was no ordinary dorm room.

"Holy smoke. You said the unit is unoccupied? Is this faculty housing?" Kevin raised a brow. There was a perpetual shortage of housing on campus; the fact that such a plummy set-up would go vacant seemed suspicious in itself.

"It's used for short-term visiting faculty," Dory said. "It's not unusual for a unit like this to sit empty for a semester. These people come in for short stays from all over the world. It can be a real pain in the ass. Very fancy people, but they can barely speak English half the time."

She pointed to the opposite wall. "That's where the picture is supposed to be. It was on loan from the museum. That's why I called you guys – that, and the fact that the bed sheets were fouled."

"Fouled?"

"Yeah." She paused for dramatic effect. "There was shit in the bed sheets. Disgusting. My crew cleaned it up."

She confirmed that everything else was in order, nothing damaged or disturbed. Kevin snapped a few photos of the room, including the empty space on the wall, then suggested they step outside for a cigarette. It was his signature investigative move. Something about the hunched posture of smoking in peripheral corners of the campus could forge a kind of kinship. It loosened up people's tongues. So Kevin and Dory stood ten feet from the building entrance near a park bench, free hands stuffed in their pockets, while he asked a few follow-up questions.

"Has there been any previous unexplained activity?" he asked.

"No; I run a tight ship." She said this as if by rote, with neither pride nor defensiveness. He noticed her cigarette was already half-gone – either she was a speed-smoker or eager to get back to that People magazine. Or maybe she was just one of those people who get nervous around cops.

"It's good that you called it in," Kevin reassured her. "Have there been any other recent break-ins in the building?" To this question, she glared at him through her eyebrows.

"I think I just answered that."

"How often do you change the locks?" he asked, trying a different tack.

"University policy states that we change the locks every five years. We should be using those new keypads, but nobody asks the supers."

It was getting chilly just standing there, and Kevin had to admit his signature move wasn't yielding any magic this time. A long ash hung suspended from Dory's spent cigarette. Time was up.

As he dropped his butt and used the steel toe of his shoe to grind it out, Dory nodded toward a passing student and said, "Oh, there's that girl again…She comes by a lot but she doesn't live here. Not sure what business she has here. You should check her out." It wasn't much of a lead, but then again, he was in no hurry to get back to HQ, and the girl had just entered the warmth of the Waverly entry hall.

"OK, thanks. I'll be in touch." Kevin double-timed it and found the girl sitting on the marble steps inside the foyer, tapping away at her phone. Closer up, he could see she looked older than an undergraduate, her brown hair swept into a loose knot below a knit cap.

He cleared his throat. "Excuse me, Miss. Detective Kevin Conley of the Campus Police. I'm investigating a recent break-in at this building. Mind if I ask you a few questions?"

She looked up at him, taking in his bulk and uniform with mild, innocent curiosity. "Sure. But I don't live here."

"Are you meeting someone who lives here?" She

nodded. "Which apartment?"

"12C."

Kevin was careful not to react. "Are you a student here?"

"I'm a grad student, international policy."

"Mind if I see your ID?" She reached into her backpack, looking slightly annoyed as she handed it over. "What, am I a suspect in some horrible crime?" She smiled with the confidence of someone whose young life had been free of such suspicions.

Kevin smiled back, he hoped winningly. "Just covering all the bases, thanks." He studied the information on her ID. Amanda Herring. Graduate Student, Arts & Sciences, good likeness in the photo. He handed it back.

"The thing is, Amanda, no one lives in 12C."

She looked surprised, but then a light came over her face. "I knew it! Last time I told him I didn't think it was really his place. Too much like a stage set. And no stuff, like laundry or dirty mugs or... a *comb*. But he insisted, and anyway, he had keys. So whatever."

"Who is your friend again?"

She squinted up at him as if she had just remembered he was still there and then abruptly stood, gathering her backpack and buttoning up her coat. "Oh shoot, I'm late for class over on the other end of campus. Okay if I go?"

"I'll walk with you. I'm headed that way." Amanda didn't look thrilled at the prospect, but she shrugged and pushed open the entry door. She kept her head down as they strode along the path together. Kevin struggled to match her brisk pace. Maybe she was trying to lose him.

"When was the last time you and your friend were there?"

"I really don't remember. Seriously, am I like a suspect?"

"Amanda, I'm doing an investigation and part of that process is asking a lot of questions to anyone in the vicinity – anyone who might have seen or heard anything."

"Well, I don't know anything. I've only been over to this part of campus a few times."

"With your friend in 12C."

"Right," she confirmed.

"And what were you doing there?" A sideways glance revealed her flushed face. Ah, he thought.

"We were just hanging out. I don't see how that matters."

"Well, again, the break-in was in that area, and as part of my investigation I'm trying to learn anything I can."

"Sorry, I don't know anything. OK, I'm headed this way. Good luck with your investigation."

She veered off onto the first fork in the path. He watched, frustrated, as she walked away. A few steps further, he saw her pull out her phone to text, slowing her pace just a little. She had been waiting for someone, and in all likelihood, she was making a plan to meet him somewhere else. Mr. Mysterious 12C. Kevin tucked his cap under his arm and stepped up onto the raised threshold of the chapel, where he had a clear view of the quad through the dappled sunlight. He leaned against a pillar, out of sight and out of the wind, as Amanda reached the grand steps of Burgess Hall and sat down to wait, pulling her red jacket closed and jamming her hands deep into her pockets.

Within a few minutes, a tall figure in a classic trench coat approached and she rose to greet him. Whoa. It was James Fensbridge, retired Member of Parliament in Canada and now a much-admired history professor. Kevin had seen him on CNN, giving his opinion on the upcoming election or some other matter of national importance. He often served as the urbane, witty emcee at university functions – he had a light touch with the donors and other VIPs.

To the casual observer, it looked like Amanda and

Fensbridge were having a simple cordial conversation. But to Kevin's trained eye, Amanda's stiff shoulders and deeply buried hands hinted at some intensity. Kevin slid carefully behind the pillar as Fensbridge surveyed the area. After maybe forty-five seconds, the professor looked at his watch. Touching the girl's arm in a gesture of polite dismissal, he walked on. Amanda stared after him, then hoisted her backpack and strode off in the other direction, shaking her head. Kevin waited until both had disappeared in the autumn afternoon glow to step out again and return to the station.

Kevin heard a snap and looked down to see that he had leaned too hard on the charcoal while his thoughts had ranged over Fensbridge and Amanda, stolen art, and, for fuck's sake, the phrase "fouled bedsheets" playing on repeat in his mind. *Dammit*, he thought, surveying his smeared image. The instructor announced the break and all the students leaned back, exchanging glances that ranged from sheepish to bored as the model shuffled into a robe, stretched, and wandered out of the room. The students stretched in much the same way and reached for their phones.

Kevin stepped out the side door for a cigarette but found the old guy in his robe already there, sucking on something home-rolled. Sharing a smoke with the recently naked figure model was too awkward, so he simply nodded and continued around the building, coming upon the familiar set of downward stairs and the green "Building Office" sign. It was like the universe was conspiring to keep the case on his mind.

His father had always said, "Break it down. You can only follow one lead at a time." As Kevin smoked, leaning on the stairwell's iron railing, he made tomorrow's plan of action: first, he would call the museum to learn more about the missing artwork (did they even know it was missing?). He would google Fensbridge – he was a public figure, so there might be some whiff of scandal or just some useful background. He would pull a list of 12C's recent tenants, and finally, he would need to write up a report for Mulally.

The heavy thunk of a door closing nearby signaled that break was ending. Kevin sighed as he stubbed out his cigarette.

"One lead at a time," he muttered to himself, determined that for tonight he would refocus on the task at hand: doing justice to the life journey etched in that man's wrinkly shanks with each charcoal stroke. There was plenty of time tomorrow for the investigation. Another benefit of doing detective work on campus was that most things just weren't that urgent. He had the luxury of moving slowly.

Chapter 2 - Glenhurst

Planning ahead wasn't one of Chief Mulally's strong suits. One of the new guys on the force had just gotten married and was heading off on a weeklong destination honeymoon. The new guy Paolo was one of those friendly, chatty people, and he'd been grumble-bragging for weeks about the drama of planning a wedding and his struggle to keep his bride and his mother from killing each other. When he gave that topic a rest, he went on about the great deal he got on the trip to Aruba. Everybody knew about the honeymoon, but somehow Mulally hadn't made a plan to cover his absence.

So Wednesday was a bad day at HQ. Mulally had surprised them all with a new duty schedule. It was right after the morning huddle. They had just done the wrap chant – Kevin didn't like to admit he loved saying the school's motto in unison: "Truth. Light. Learning." Then they would clap once and disperse. But today, Mulally added a little flourish to the event.

"Congratulations to Paolo on his big day. Since he'll be away, I've had to move some assignments around. I'll post them on the wall; you can also see them in the online scheduler. I appreciate your flexibility in advance." He pressed his beefy fists into the table, easing his bulk from the swivel chair, and walked slowly to the bulletin board. A couple people followed him over to look at the schedule on the wall; Kevin and Rafiq returned to their desks and checked online.

Everybody had to take a turn on Paolo's shitty shifts, even the detectives. There was a lot of moaning; they were all in a foul mood. Kevin was especially irritated to find he'd been placed on night shift for a week, starting tomorrow. He leaned into Mulally's office to object, but Mulally just shrugged and said, "Life isn't fair, Conley. I gotta take into account people's family obligations and a shit ton of other factors you don't even want to know about. You'll make it work. I know I can count on you."

The flattery was not lost on Kevin. Of course, he'd be the one who had to make it work. With no spouse and no kids, almost anyone's needs took precedence over his own. He returned to his desk, dropping into his seat with an exaggerated groan.

Rafiq leaned over from his adjacent desk and muttered, "Last week, I offered to put the schedule together for him – I could see this coming. Nope, he said, he had it under control."

Kevin tried to smile, "Well, at least we're on duty together a few of those nights."

"Yeah, man. And now I gotta call Marie and tell her I won't be doing bath and story time for a week. Wish me luck." He reached for his phone. "Don't worry man, we'll make the best of it."

The schedule change meant Kevin had to put his investigation on hold. That kind of detective work couldn't be done at night in between breaking up parties and walking the quad. He would miss drawing class next Tuesday, and he would have to reschedule his planned visit to Glenhurst to tonight even though the prospect filled him with dread. As he glumly considered his options, his email inbox pinged with an automated notification from the residential care home. No critical news on his mother, just the universe piling on with a pro forma message saying that his "family member" would be happy to see him.

Glenhurst was ten miles out of his way, and he headed there straight after work, clenching his teeth and trying to remember when he had last made the trip. It had been at least two weeks, maybe three. He told himself he had been busy. He had made a pact with himself to start dating again, and somehow the idea of opening the dating apps had become linked to visiting his mother at Glenhurst, then prioritized, then procrastinated over, and then both had fallen off the to-do list entirely. Kevin chewed on the inside of his cheek, reflecting on the problem with self-improvement plans.

He took a deep breath and consciously relaxed his grip on the steering wheel, stretching his jaw to release the dull ache building there. He gave himself a pep talk as he pulled into the familiar parking lot on its undesirable sliver of real estate – the place was practically encircled by an interstate access ramp. As he switched off the ignition, he glanced at himself in the rearview mirror, hoping to see his game face. He rearranged his features, stretching his cheeks into a smile and massaging the crease in his forehead until it faded.

Kevin stepped out of the car and went around to the trunk, where he pulled off his service belt and changed into running shoes. He zipped a red track jacket over his uniform; it was the color he'd worn in high school. He picked up his spiral sketch pad and a little grocery bag and tucked them under his arm. In no particular hurry, he turned toward the fake portico entrance of the bland three-story building. As the automatic door slid open, the air conditioning expelled a draft that smelled like senility, with notes of broiled chicken, antiseptic spray, dandruff, and urine. He rolled his neck and shoulders and kept walking down the slate blue hallway, its sides discreetly flanked by safety rails. Room 342 looked just the same. Recliner, dresser, side table, and an adjustable bed with a crocheted coverlet neatly folded across the end. Mary Conley sat upright in the recliner, facing the window and the dusky view of a few scrubby pines outside. The highway was loud even with the windows closed. Kevin walked into her sight line and leaned in for a crooked hug.

"Hi Mom, how are you?" His voice, even to him, sounded like a weak imitation of his father's bantering tone.

His mother slowly turned her face up to look at him and said, "What seems to be the trouble, Officer?" *Goddamn gabardine slacks*, thought Kevin. He reached into his left pocket and jingled his keys, an old nervous habit.

"It's me, Mom - Kevin. There's no trouble; I'm just stopping in to see how you're doing." He set his things down on the coverlet and perched on the edge of the bed facing her chair. She turned her gaze back to the window.

"My son worked with the campus police. I haven't seen him in a long time; I think he was killed in action. Are you here to tell me what happened?"

"No Mom – that's me. I'm Kevin, your son. I'm right here." Not for the first time, he found himself wanting to shake her, or shout into her face, or just run from the room in despair. Not for the first time, he held his ground and held the smile on his face as he repeated, "I'm your son, Kevin."

"After his father died, he stopped visiting. I can't blame him. Who would want to come here?"

And right on cue, a sharp wailing started from the next room. Kevin heard the soft squeak of white shoes as someone went in, followed by the fake cheerfulness of nurses everywhere narrating the situation for a helpless patient. "Oh, let's see what's happening here Essie. Can't reach your juice cup? Here you go! Now that's not so bad, is it? Let's plump up your pillows a bit and get you straightened up. That's great. Doesn't your hair look pretty today?"

Kevin's mother was still ruminating. "He was a good boy. Not the brightest, but good-hearted. I wonder if he ever got married – he must be 25 by now. A good time to settle down." She sighed and paused, eyes still facing the window. Turning slightly, she said, "What seems to be the trouble, Officer?"

"No trouble, Mom. Just me, Kevin, here for a visit. How about we read a little?" Thirty-six years old, he reached for the book on the nightstand – it was Robert Service poems. He opened it at random, cleared his throat and started reading aloud.

> Ye who know the Lone Trail
> fain would follow it,
> Though it lead to glory
> or the darkness of the pit.
>
> Ye who take the Lone Trail,
> bid your love good-by;
> The Lone Trail, the Lone Trail
> follow till you die.

"Sometimes it's better just to be quiet." His mother said. Given the mournful tone of the poem, Kevin had to agree. He closed the book. He wasn't sure if he was supposed to be completely quiet, or just stop reading. After a few minutes, he remembered the bag of Twizzlers.

"I brought you some of the candy you like." His mother nodded at the window. Kevin pulled the bright package from the bag and placed it in the drawer of her nightstand. "I'll just leave them in the drawer for you." He vigorously crumpled the brown bag and tossed it, hoops-style, toward the waste bin. "Score!" he peeled, as the bag sailed in. Mary nodded slowly; her gaze still trained on the window.

He reached for his pad and started sketching. At the top right corner, he neatly wrote the date. Then he tried to draw the woman he saw in front of him, not the one he remembered. He struggled to render the drooping skin below the eyes, and to really see the veiny, milky-white skin where his mother's ruddy forearms used to be, when they were dappled with freckles and fine ginger hair, laughing and lifting her boy up to rest on her hip and give him a quick kiss on his smooth cheek.

The slippers were toughest of all. In his drawing, Kevin wanted to give her real shoes, maybe the penny loafers he remembered, so that she could jump up like she used to, saying, "*Who wants scallion pancakes?*" and hustle them all off to Shu Ming on Main Street for Chinese. She would give him the umbrella from her tiki cocktail and tease laughter from his father. If it was a good night, his dad would relax enough to ask for extra pineapple slices with dessert, "so there'd be some left for the menfolk." She always liked that routine.

Kevin skipped the slippers and focused on her face. There was silence behind her eyes. The room was so still.

After twenty minutes or so, he closed his pad and got up.

"Well, mom, I need to hit the road. I have a busy week coming up at work. It's great to see you."

"Good to see you, Officer. If you see my son, tell him he should come visit. That is, if he still lives here. I think he might have moved away."

Kevin swallowed hard. "I will, ma'am. I'll do that. You take care." Kevin placed his hand on her bony shoulder, but she flinched as he started to lean toward her, so he backed off, his heart sinking.

He was glad the business office was dark behind its glass door. He really did not want to talk about late payments tonight. Or let's face it, any night. Back at the car, he opened the trunk, slowly tore out the sketch and threw it on the stack with the others. He rifled through the pile, scanning past more recent class drawings, to find the last one from Glenhurst. It was dated exactly a month ago.

He felt obligated to go to Glenhurst, even though it was always the same. Still, he had to go. She was so alone in her confusion, and by extension so was he. When his father died, his mother's decline had happened quickly. If your own parents don't know you, who are you? A man without a family, without a tribe. Just a guy with a condo and a job. He really needed to get this dating thing moving. Maybe if he kept at it, he could be on a trip to Aruba himself someday.

Chapter 3 - The Night Shift

"Everything OK over there, folks?" It was just after ten that Saturday night, the last night that Kevin would be walking the quad on the night shift, and in the gloom of the tall elms, he could see an odd shadow moving along the base of the Henry Moore sculpture. The shadow resolved into two people, suddenly upright. A girlish voice answered back, "Yes, sir. Everything's fine." Kevin had been careful to stand on the path under a streetlamp before he called out, so he knew they could see him clearly.

"Maybe time to head home, then," he said, thinking better of the idea of reproaching them for getting nasty on a valuable work of art. As he walked on, he pictured the undulating curves of the sculpture in his mind's eye and wondered if Moore had maybe designed the piece with exactly that activity in mind.

Things had been quiet all week, but the weekend was always a wild card on campus. It was strict policy that uniformed officers would walk the rounds. Main quad, science quad, dorms, west campus, an hour back at HQ to warm up and drink some coffee, then go around again. It was pretty tame stuff and frankly, boring. Kevin seesawed between finding the students' collective cluelessness charming and finding it completely maddening. Yesterday, for instance. Walking through the housing quad around midnight, he had come across a girl lying on a bench, her left arm dangling so that the back of her hand scraped the sidewalk. As Kevin approached, the stench of beer vomit hit him, and he could see the girl's hand was resting in a puddle of puke. Gingerly, he leaned over and shook her by the shoulder. The kid's eyes fluttered, and she said, "My keys are in my pocket. Parker Commons 214." Parker was a freshman dorm. Now that Kevin was sure she was okay, he took an extra minute to consider her there, lying so helpless and exposed with her gold hoodie and fuzzy slippers. He wondered if this was what her parents had in mind when they packed up the SUV and proudly delivered her to the university.

As gently as he could, Kevin got her on her feet, holding her limp arm over his shoulders and supporting her with his other arm around her waist. She was no more than five feet tall – she probably weighed a hundred pounds of pure cluelessness.

"What's your name?" he asked, hoping to get her talking. They were about an eight-minute walk from Parker Commons on the opposite corner of the quad.

"Annabelle," she said, "What's yours?"

"Kevin. Let's get you home. Looks like you had quite a party tonight."

"Yeah. It was SO FUN. But then I noticed my friends had left, and I was walking home, and a felt a little dizzy so I sat down on that bench…" She gestured vaguely behind them, "What party poopers." She stumbled a little; Kevin propped her back on her feet.

"Yeah, friends should stick together," he agreed.

"You smell good." Awkward, Kevin thought, and he certainly couldn't return the compliment.

"Is that…aftershave? You smell like a dad." She nestled against his shoulder.

"Nope, not a dad," he said, "Just a community service officer. We'll get you home."

Kevin used his access card to open the entry door for Parker Commons, then looked up the RA on the bulletin board. He dialed her number on his cell. Fortunately, she came right down, wrapped in a flannel bathrobe.

"Anabelle!" she called out, sounding like an exasperated older sister. Her British accent made the name sound less ridiculous.

"Hi Tory. What a fun party – you should have come!" In the light of the entryway, Annabelle looked even more disheveled. Bits of oak leaf clung to her hoodie and her hair. Her eyes were almost closed; her head tipped forty-five degrees to the left. She reached out as if to give Tory a hug.

"Annabelle!" Tory spoke more sharply. "Please thank this kind police officer for walking you home."

"Police ossifer?" Annabelle turned squarely to face Kevin for the first time, taking in his CAMPO uniform. She giggled and covered her mouth. "Uh oh. I think I am in trouble now."

"We'll worry about that tomorrow. Let's get you cleaned up and into bed. Hopefully you'll have a truly massive hangover tomorrow and it will be a lesson to you." Tory turned to thank Kevin; he handed her his card and asked that she email tomorrow to let him know how Annabelle was feeling. They could discuss what kind of report to file.

Kevin left the building shaking his head. Annabelle's evening could have gone so much worse. Did these kids live under some kind of magical protective spell? A little headache maybe, and she probably wouldn't even remember being walked home by a campus cop.

Tonight, Kevin was back at HQ draining coffee from his mug, about to take another loop of the grounds, when a young guy in that same gold hoodie walked in. Kevin looked up, "Can I help you?" The kid looked around shyly, and said, "No, everything's fine. I was just walking by and realized I'd never been in here before. I saw your lights on."

"Yeah," says Kevin. "There's always someone here. Pretty quiet tonight for a Friday."

"You look familiar," said the kid, scrutinizing Kevin's face. He framed his fingers into the shape of a cropping box and looked through them at Kevin, who recognized the gesture from art class. "I know" – he said, "you're in my figure drawing class. You're a hook lefty."

Kevin was taken aback. He always imagined himself invisible in class, maybe because he himself wasn't paying much attention to the other students. Some detective. The boy in front of him was wholly unfamiliar: pale and slender, with Clark Kent glasses, and a mass of unwashed curly hair.

"I think you're right," he said. "How do you like the class?"

"It's good," the kid pushed his glasses up tight against the bridge of his nose, then stuffed his hands back into his pockets. "It's tough to get it right, but I like it. How about you? I never thought about someone being a cop and an artist before."

Kevin nodded, thinking, I never thought about someone being a student and dropping by a police station for no reason on a Saturday night before either. "Want some coffee?" The boy shrugged, so Kevin got up and went to the coffee machine. "What's your name?"

"Jason."

Kevin wondered if something might be wrong, but the kid wasn't in any obvious distress, so he figured he'd just feel him out and see what came up. They sat with their coffee, asking and answering small-talky questions. It was a change of pace anyway from watching Rafiq play Red Dead Redemption in the conference room.

But, after twenty minutes of asking about Jason's major (math), other art classes (ceramics), Game of

Thrones, his hometown (Kenosha, Wisconsin), his roommates (two dudes, introduced with a shrug), Kevin still had no bead on why he had wandered in. Maybe just lonely? Unfortunately, it was time to do another lap of the campus.

And then the fire whistle started blaring. Shit. He and Rafiq would have to go together. Ninety percent of fire alerts on campus were false alarms, and the main job of the campus cops was to create a buffer between the students (clueless) and the firefighters (busy professionals with millions of dollars of equipment and the excess machismo that comes with it). When he got to the annunciator near the HQ entrance, Rafiq was already there.

"Looks like Hollister."

"They don't have the new system yet, do they?"

"Nope." They noticed an intermittent signal on the board, but it didn't change the procedure. They grabbed their hats to go; Jason walked out with them and waved good luck. Kevin's last thought on Jason was that he would probably see him hovering around the gathering crowd at Hollister in a few minutes. It's hard to resist the gawker urge at a fire, especially when you've already established that you've got nothing better to do. As they jogged toward the dorms, Rafiq asked, "I wonder what caused the blink on the signal?" They could hear the fire truck sirens a block or so away; that was good news. Their buffering duties worked better when they could arrive first. As they rounded the corner of the building, it was easy to see where the problem was – people in every stage of undress were gathered outside the main entrance to Hollister. A student, her voice slightly annoyed but mostly indifferent, said, "It's a false alarm, third floor," and held the door open for them. Kevin and Rafiq, seeing no sign of smoke, trotted in.

As they rounded the landing to the second floor, Kevin noticed that the usual dorm odor of cement and dirty socks had been replaced by something more like a barber shop married to a Macy's perfume counter. Cloying sweet, minty, and fruity aromas. Rafiq slipped as they turned the corner for the last flight of steps, and as Kevin reached out to steady him, they both slowed down and looked around. The featureless walls were streaked with white foam and drippy pastel goo in every shade. There was green foam on the stair skids – hence the slipping. Foam was smeared on the handrails. The place was deserted and eerily quiet. As they peered around the corner of the stairwell, into the long hallway on the third floor, the foam was everywhere. White, green, even blue. Golden gooey streaks dripped down the walls, as if Jackson Pollack had been there. Empty shampoo bottles, tubes, and aluminum cannisters littered the linoleum. Two hundred feet down the hall, they saw a figure clinging awkwardly to the wall. What the hell? They approached cautiously; the perp watched them coming. Rafiq ran his fingers through one of the smears on the wall and sniffed.

"Shaving cream," he murmured.

"Excellent detective work, Sherlock," Kevin replied quietly. The guy appeared to be a student; their training made them approach with caution. Passing a large yellow wall splatter, Kevin smelled factory-grade lemon scent.

The kid clinging to the wall was wearing gym shorts and a torn t-shirt. But mostly he was wearing what Kevin's barber euphemistically called "product." He was literally covered in shaving cream. His hair was sticking up in stiff spikes, coated with green and white foam. His clothes were transparent in patches where the viscous stuff had soaked through. He was shivering.

"What's going on here, son?" asked Kevin.

"Uh, well Officer, we were having a little shaving cream fight. And somebody hit the alarm by accident. We noticed that when we hold up the lever, the alarm stops. So I'm holding up the lever."

"Let go for a second," said Kevin. The kid looked relieved and let go. Immediately, the piercing din was unbearable." "Hold it up! Hold it up!" Kevin and Rafiq hollered. The kid resumed his original awkward position, leaning into the wall and pressing up the tiny lever as if it held his destiny. It took another second for the ringing to stop in their ears.

"The fire crew is on their way. They'll reset the system," said Rafiq. "Stay here. What's your name?"

"Ted Sevilla," the kid said, looking down.

Kevin and Rafiq turned and jogged back toward the stairwell, giving each other sidelong glances. The whole place was still deserted. As soon as they turned the corner and were out of sight of the kid, they doubled over silently laughing.

"Holy shit, Ted Sevilla!" said Rafiq.

"I wish I could have taken a picture; no one will believe it."

"Ted Sevilla is my fucking hero." Rafiq chortled. "Everyone else deserted him like a pack of rats."

"OK, we need to go meet the truck; give the all-clear. They are not going to like this." Kevin was the ranking officer; they needed to reestablish their game faces.

They passed through the entry doors just as the fire chief arrived and briefed them on the situation. Of course, the fire fighters would conduct an independent review, and of course it would take time. Kevin couldn't help noticing that among the students milling around outside, no one had a dollop of shaving cream on them. The rats had run off to hide in friends' rooms around the quad, no doubt, laying low until the authorities moved on – underscoring the heroism of Ted Sevilla, who would take the rap alone.

When the shift ended at 1:00 am, Rafiq asked if Kevin wanted to grab a quick beer before last call. They changed out of their uniforms and found two empty stools at a townie bar on Main. They ordered drafts just as the barkeep announced last call. Rafiq proposed a toast to Fuckin' Ted Sevilla, and they laughed with respect at the memory of his skinny, sopping wet sacrifice.

"These kids," said Rafiq. "They can make you crazy. My son is five…sometimes I try to keep him in mind when the students do something super stupid, or just plain goofy. I hope someone will take pity on him when he gets to be an idiot teenager away from home."

Kevin shook his head. "Remember that kid who came to HQ to lodge a complaint against his roommate?"

"Oh right - the guy who wouldn't shower. The kid said he thought it was 'criminal behavior.' He wanted us to show up in full uniform, hands on holsters, and escort the kid to the shower while we read his Miranda rights."

They laughed at their beers.

Rafiq, still looking at his beer, asked Kevin, "You still taking those art classes?"

"Sure, why?"

"I'm just trying to figure out what's next. You've been here, what, six years? I'm going on four, and I still haven't made detective. It's OK here, but I'm not sure. I feel itchy. I'm about due to take the civil service exam again, trying to get on the city force. Are you still trying for it?"

"Funny you should ask. I just realized the last time I went up was right before my dad died. That was like three years ago. Noticing that, it made me wonder if being on the city force was his dream more than mine. I like it here…I like being around the kids, the rhythm of the seasons. I like the art classes…I'll finish up with a master's degree next year."

"No shit! Are you gonna become an art teacher or something?"

"No, I'm not looking for a career change."

Kevin realized, as he said it, that it was true. Whatever restlessness he felt, it wasn't about his job. But still he decided to change the subject. "I feel like I still have something to learn from Mulally."

Rafiq's eyebrows jumped up as he scoffed, "He's washed up, just clocking in for a few extra years before he retires off to Florida or something."

Kevin nodded at his glass. "He does seem to move in slow motion most days. But I see these little glimmers of wisdom…I wish I could map out the thought process going on inside his bald head. It's like he's seeing more dimensions in the map, if you know what I mean."

"The dude's obsessed with filing reports," Rafiq griped. Kevin guffawed.

"That's the truth. But I've been listening to cops complain about paperwork since I was a kid, so I don't think we can pin that on Mulally."

"Hey, what was up with that sad sack kid from earlier…no better plans on a Saturday night?"

Kevin had nearly forgotten about Jason. Now he shrugged. "Not sure. Nice enough kid. Math major."

Rafiq snorted, "Man, I never could hack math. Even the stats we had to take at the police academy nearly did me in."

"I hear you," Kevin agreed. "Turns out he's in my art class."

"You've got a stalker?"

"No, I don't think so – I think it's a just a small campus coincidence." Kevin drained his glass. "Well, man, it's been nice catching up but I'm not gonna lie. I'll be happy to be back on days next week."

"I hear you, man. I'm too old for this late-night shit." They grabbed their jackets and headed their separate ways at the door.

Chapter 4 – Stakeout

The following Monday, Kevin was back on his regular schedule, warming up to the next steps in his art theft investigation.

After his first cup of coffee, he called the museum and asked to speak with the curator of etchings. After a few rings, someone picked up.

"Artemis Johns," spoke a low voice, throaty like an old movie vixen. Kevin was suddenly tongue-tied and stammered through an explanation of who he was and why he was calling.

"My word," she said. "Let me pull up the records on the piece. Hold for a moment please."

While he waited, he sketched what he imagined she looked like. Trench coat, vivid lipstick, fedora pulled down low. Lots of shadows around her legs. The quick drawing made her look like Carmen Sandiego.

The voice came back on the line. "Artist Joseph Marie Vien, French, 18th century. It was due to be returned next month. How bizarre that it has disappeared; it's not especially valuable, and this sort of etching is quite out of vogue right now."

"So you don't think there was a strong financial incentive for a theft?"

"Not at all," she confirmed. "But, you know, people love souvenirs from the university. Maybe it was something in that line. A little prank – someone can hang it on their wall at home and chuckle over their little act of transgression and derring-do."

Kevin asked her to send over a digital image of the piece. She did so immediately, with the thumbnail attachment appearing in his inbox before they had rung off. He told her they would continue to investigate and keep her updated with any progress. She thanked him and sighed, "I suppose I'll have to report the loss to our insurance company."

"Yes, and if you need a police report for that, just give me a call."

"Maybe I'll wait a few weeks in case your investigation turns it up?" she wondered aloud. This made Kevin like her even more – they shared a mutual avoidance of paperwork.

"I'll leave that decision in your capable hands," he chuckled. As he hung up the phone, he wondered if there might be a reason for him, at some point, to saunter over to the gallery and check in with her in person. He liked the museum; the coffee shop in the central atrium was bathed in light that was imported straight from Giverny.

Kevin grabbed another cup of coffee from the office urn. Back at his desk, he clicked on the image Artemis Johns had sent. It didn't reveal much. Then he read through the notes he had scribbled a week earlier. Mostly he was thinking about Professor Fensbridge – that part just didn't add up. He could see the appeal of having a quiet, out of the way apartment for meeting your girl on the side, and that might even fit in with the kinky stuff, but why the missing art? The guy had plenty of money and probably a house full of etchings. Even the sexy curator lady had said this one wasn't worth much. Kevin was momentarily distracted by Rafiq's voice booming over near the coffee machine, enthusiastically interrupting the new guy's honeymoon travelogue to tell him about Ted Sevilla's heroics.

Mulally ambled over to Kevin's desk clutching two old-school pink "while you were out" phone messages in his right fist.

"Didn't you go over to west campus on a theft case a couple weeks ago?"

"Yeah, why?"

"Huh. I didn't see the report. Anyway, there's another complaint from that building – it's Waverly, right? Two different neighbors called in noise/suspicious activity. Interesting that they didn't call last night - they waited until today. Why don't you go check it out."

"Whoever was making the noise is either gone, or they've slept it off."

Mulally paused and looked over his half-rims at Kevin for a beat. "Yeah. But seeing as how we are into community service policing here, and making our community members feel safe, I'm asking you to go over there and get a couple of statements from the complainants." He set the paper slips on Kevin's desk, with a stubby finger tap for emphasis.

"You got it, chief."

"Don't call me chief."

"Yes, sir." Mulally was already walking away, but he looked back and grimaced, palms up in a "really?" gesture, before shuffling into his office. Kevin glanced at his watch, then hastily turned to his screen to file the forgotten report. Short and sweet, just the missing art and the museum action items. No color commentary, no prognostications that could trip him up later. He shoved his pad in his back pocket and headed out. What with walking the campus during last week's night shift and all these trips to west campus, maybe he should get one of those fitness bracelets. Keep track of all this walking. It would justify an extra beer once a week. Or maybe he could requisition a Segway, like in that mall cop movie.

An hour later, on his return to HQ, he walked straight through the bullpen into Mulally's office with a new sense of purpose, humming from the pleasant jolt of adrenaline he got when a case was really turning into something. Both complainants were adjacent to the vacant unit – one on each side. It was too neat to be a coincidence.

"Chief, I think this noise complaint may be connected to the theft. There's something going on in that unit. I think we should put one of those motion sensor thingies in there, so we can get beeped when the perp shows up."

Mulally shook his head. "You know how hard it is to get one of those things approved around here. Did they say the noise was coming from inside the apartment?"

"They weren't sure. Just that the noise was 'unusual.' Both complaints were from apartments next door – on either side! I could do a stakeout. The empty unit is on the first floor and the windows look right out on the quad." Mulally still looked skeptical.

"For noisy neighbors? We'd be staking out every dorm on campus."

"Maybe we'll catch the thief."

"You said yourself we'll never find that crummy painting."

"Etching," Kevin mumbled. "But that was before we had evidence of, ah," he coughed, "additional suspicious activity. The perp is returning to the scene, for Christ's sake, and there's no more art in there."

"I hear you. On the other hand, Conley – unspecified *noise* in campus housing isn't exactly suspicious. The kid upstairs might have dropped his typewriter. We'll continue to monitor the situation. Write it up."

Mulally turned back toward his computer. Kevin watched his wide sloping back, frustrated, thinking, "Typewriter? Does he think this is 1980?" Why had he walked all the way over there – twice now - and taken the witness statements if they weren't going to pursue it? Did

Mulally really only care about filing the report? Kevin's gut was still buzzing with the conviction that something bigger was happening in 12C. He heard his father's voice again: *follow your hunches.*

And that was how he found himself on stakeout, although not officially on duty, later that night. He sincerely hoped that whatever was going down would happen tonight. He had class tomorrow, and since he was technically volunteering, he figured he could do it at his own convenience. He was hunkered down in his Camaro in the student lot next to Thorndike, with a clear view of the front entrance to Waverly Hall, eating a burrito wrapped in wax paper and foil and burping on fizzy warm diet coke from a plastic bottle. Sexy stuff. He watched as people went in and out of the building, flipping on light switches as they entered their apartments, and about sixty percent of the time, flipping them off when they left.

Up on the fourth floor, he saw the outline of a woman slinging a bag over her shoulder. The light went out, and a few moments later she pressed her weight against the building's exterior door and strode off, buttoning up against the cool night air, all attention focused on the phone in her hand. Ten minutes later a lanky dude acted out an identical routine from the other side of the building. It was predictable and not even remotely interesting. Maybe Mulally was right. 12C was on the first floor, last window on the right. No sign of activity there. Not yet. Crumpling up the burrito wrapper, Kevin reached for some gum.

When he looked up, two people had just reached the Waverly main entrance. A big woman led the way, closely followed by a small squirrelly guy wearing a snug beige windbreaker. The man looked furtively around before sliding through the door she held open for him. They disappeared from view. A dim light appeared in 12C, around the edges of the drawn window shades. Kevin's heart thumped; he froze. What now? He wasn't in uniform. He grabbed his badge and phone and walked toward Waverly, trying to look nonchalant, unsatisfied with what little he could see from the sidewalk. Using his pass card to enter the building, he walked slowly toward the apartment. There was a thin line of light under the door, but all was quiet. What could he really do? Mulally would flip out if he intervened, off-duty and acting alone. It was too risky. Kevin went back outside and sat on a bench tucked under a bush, just to the left of the entry door. About 20 minutes later, Squirrelly came out alone and headed to the right, shoulders hunched and hands jammed in his pockets. After another ten minutes, the woman appeared. She walked casually out the front door and turned toward Kevin. She passed right in front of him, checking her phone, so close that he could hear her breath in the quiet night, along with the click of her high heels, their tiny points straining like they would snap under her weight. She wore a big black coat with some kind of shiny gold scarf at her throat. Her nails were also painted gold, glowing in the dim light from her phone screen. She moved slowly in her trembling shoes, clicking away into the distance.

Kevin's mind raced even as his heartbeat slowly returned to normal. What was Goldfinger up to? He hadn't heard loud noises or scuffling. How did Amanda and Fensbridge fit in? When he'd stopped by earlier to ask Dory about the noise complaint, she'd brushed him off. Neither of these two looked like visiting faculty, that much was certain. He had to get a motion-sensor alarm in there, maybe even a surveillance camera. He needed to know what was going on. He had to persuade Mulally, and he needed to do it all very quietly so no one got tipped off.

He stayed on the bench, not ready to leave, even though he had accomplished his mission. He lit a cigarette and sat with it, rocking a little, leaning forward with his elbows on his knees as he tried to piece it together. He now knew for sure that someone was using the suite. What for? An affair? It seemed more like some kind of commercial transaction – maybe drugs? But what about the *fouled bedsheets*. Who were these two? The place was starting to feel like Grand Central Station. Squirrely had looked guilty as hell, but Goldfinger couldn't have been more nonchalant. It didn't add up – which usually meant he had a real case on his hands.

Kevin smiled as he noticed that he'd given the subjects nicknames. It was another old trick of his father's – the descriptive names added color to the gray work of investigation. He found himself quoting his dad out loud, *"If it doesn't add up, you're missing an entry."* But there was nothing left to learn tonight, so Kevin ground the cigarette under his steel toe and headed back to the car.

Arriving home later that night, he was still keyed up. He wanted to do something productive; he was filled with resolve. Kevin had a superstitious faith in lucky streaks, and he had the feeling he might be starting one. He snapped open his laptop on the dining table and logged into Hinge. It had been a while and there was a backlog. He grabbed a beer from the fridge and challenged himself: he would commit to looking for matches until the beer was gone. He would contact at least three. Right away he saw a couple that might work out. One was a round-faced, smiling woman who described herself as an artist; the other was a ginger-haired nurse who liked movies and baseball. Both pretty, but not trying too hard. Kevin sent them both messages, his usual short and sweet, "Love your bio, are you willing to have a chat?" and then scanned through a bunch more. The longer he scanned, the more he found red flags in the women's profiles. This one was too skinny, that one had a guilty expression. Too much eye make-up (what was she hiding?). Another worked in a dry cleaner, and he imagined a strange chemical aroma clinging to her hair. Plus dry cleaners were notorious for money laundering.

He raised his beer bottle again. Discovering it was empty, he decided to declare victory at two. Scratching at the paper label on the neck of the bottle, Kevin's thoughts returned to how he would craft his surveillance pitch to Mulally. He felt sure that he needed to catch the perps in the act, whatever it was. Feeling strong, he dropped to the floor and did twenty quick push-ups, imagining how his biceps might look to a ginger-haired nurse.

Back at headquarters the next day, the persuasion part turned out to be easier than expected. Kevin walked into the office after running some morning rounds to find Mulally waiting for him. "Step into my office, Conley."

"What'd you do after work last night?" Buying time, Kevin mimicked one of Mulally's own noncommittal gestures – shrug, eyebrows, hands wide. This was definitely not just idle chit chat. Mulally wasn't that kind of boss.

"I got a call this morning from that building manager…Florie or whatsername."

Kevin nodded, trying to look pensive.

"She's a piece of work. She wondered why you were parked on a bench outside Waverly around nine. I'm curious too."

Kevin decided to stick with the slow nodding while he covered his surprise at learning that Dory had been surveilling him while he surveilled Waverly Hall. He was thinking a cigarette would be good.

"Like I said, I'm curious too. But I'm more curious about why she gives a shit about who is sitting on a public bench on an open campus, at a time when she's off-duty."

This both surprised and delighted Kevin. It was one of those flashes of wisdom he'd been telling Rafiq about – one of those moments when Mulally could sense a bigger pattern and grab hold of a case. Kevin spied the vestiges of the hungry investigator Mulally had been, back when he'd led internal affairs in the force over in Bethesda. Before he'd semi-retired ten years ago to life at CAMPO. Kevin's face broke into a wide smile.

"So what did you see? Let's break it down."

Kevin relayed the story, bit by bit, stringing out the details along with his nicknames and the hypotheses he'd formed. He could see Mulally mentally totting up the risks.

"These people did not look like they belonged here. They are using the apartment for something shady," Kevin wrapped it up.

"Fencing? This whole thing started with a theft."

"They didn't seem to be carrying anything…"

"Could be small…jewelry, flash drives, drugs. They were in there for, what, you said twenty minutes? Could be trafficking/sex trade. What else do you know?"

Kevin told him about the pretty student – Amanda, and the professor. Mulally whistled when he heard Fensbridge's name.

"That guy. He's a ticking Title IX bomb. Politicians are always up to something slimy. Looks like you've got yourself a real juicy case. I want you to proceed cautiously – let's keep the super out of the loop. My gut tells me she's bent." Kevin nodded. He wasn't as sure, but he had a general bias to distrust lifers who seemed too comfortable in their work. Or put another way, exactly how bent? Cadging toilet paper or something much bigger?

Mulally continued, "And speaking of the super, she tossed some suspicion on the cleaning crew." Kevin groaned. "I know, classic misdirection. But, to keep her calm, you're going to have to follow up that lead."

"Agreed. Obnoxious but necessary."

"Good work, Conley." Mulally nodded and turned to his screen, signaling that it was time for Kevin to depart. As he rose and let himself out, it was all Kevin could do not to whistle. As he passed Rafiq's desk, he reached out for a high five.

"What are we celebrating?" Rafiq asked, slapping his hand and following it with a fist bump.

"Just life, man. Life is good."

And so the wheels were in motion for the motion sensor alarm in apartment 12C. Kevin checked the class schedule too, figuring he might change clothes and go sit in the back row of Fensbridge's three o'clock lecture "Public Goods in the Modern Polity," just to get an eyeball on the guy. He was on the trail.

And just as he was putting the last details in his stakeout report, which of course Mulally had reminded him to do when he walked through the bullpen for a refill, Kevin's phone pinged with a response from Hinge. It was from the artist – the one with the round face and the nice smile. Sheila. She wrote back suggesting that, with their shared interest in art, maybe he would like to meet her at PaintBar. He frowned. PaintBar was one of those places where groups of middle-aged women would go to drink wine and make identical acrylic paintings. He couldn't decide if it was a terrible or an awesome idea. On the one hand, something to do with your hands, something to look at, a task. On the other hand, the scheduled class was two hours long and what if she was terrible. Or what if she obviously thought he was terrible. Plus cheesy acrylic paintings – they would probably have to paint pumpkins or a cartoon witch, given the time of year. He chided himself for overthinking - her message was a reassuring sign that he was indeed on a lucky streak. He messaged back, confirming the date and time and then reached out to Buildings & Grounds to figure out where the cleaning crew would be this afternoon. He decided not to google or stalk Sheila online. Past experience suggested that stuff would just make you crazy. He would approach this date the old-fashioned way, with no reviews or ratings, just two people spending a little time together in a well-lit public place to see if they hit it off. He would channel his curiosity about Sheila into figuring out how Goldfinger, Fensbridge, and Reinaldo the cleaning supervisor were connected.

That same day, early in the evening, Kevin was hunched again in the sketching chair with an arrowhead of charcoal staining the side of his thumb. This time the subject was a damn golden retriever. What, did all the naked human models leave town for the holiday? He struggled to carve the waves of swirling fur, thinking his own hand was as useless as the paw he was failing to render.

At the break, the kid who had stopped by police headquarters on Saturday night wandered over to bum a cigarette. "Jason, right? You're too young to smoke," Kevin said as he held out his pack. He had been ruminating on his interview with Reinaldo Reyes. Jason seemed happy to smoke silently, so Kevin continued his puzzling.

The cleaning crew had been scheduled to move through the student center around 2:00 pm. Kevin had a photo ID of the crew chief, so he had gotten a cup of coffee and sat down to wait for the guy. He hoped to catch him by surprise. Twenty minutes to spare, give or take. He pulled out his sketch pad and tried to reproduce the elaborate pattern on the carpet at his feet. Good practice, but it was tough to concentrate when he had to monitor every passerby for a positive ID. Right on time, a stocky dark-haired guy with an alert gaze walked by – he looked like a man going places.

Kevin stood, "Reinaldo?" The man paused with a smile. "Yes, can I help you?" His English was accented but clear.

Kevin flashed his university police badge and said, "Do you have a few minutes?"

37

The smile faded as Reinaldo looked at his watch. "Just a few. We are on a tight schedule. What's this about?" He looked serious, but not agitated.

"We had a theft over in Waverly Hall."

"Ah." Reinaldo's expression revealed both relief and a measure of defiance. Kevin knew from his own experience that suspicion always fell first on the cleaning crew, and that it was almost never justified.

"That painting, right? We reported it when we noticed it was missing."

"Right. Have you had any other recent experiences of missing items?"

Reinaldo's eyes narrowed. "My team is solid. No one would risk their job to take some small thing. I know all these people well – they work here for ten years, even more."

"Right, right. Of course. I'm not suspecting your crew. There's just been a few different strange things over there at Waverly, and Dory Johnson suggested we talk to you as part of our investigation, in case you've noticed anything unusual."

At Dory's name, Reinaldo's demeanor changed abruptly. His lips tightened; Kevin watched his chest rise and fall as he took two long, deep breaths. He could see Reinaldo weighing his words.

Kevin asked again, "Have you noticed anything unusual over there?"

"I notice she loses a lot of papers and I have to do double work to get my people paid. I notice she doesn't lift her fingers but criticizes others for many things. I notice she docks my pay for lost keys when no keys are lost. This is a great university, but not all the peoples are great."

"So you don't get along."

Reinaldo regained his equanimity, showing his teeth in an imitation smile. "I get along with all the supers. That's my job. I run a good crew, keep the buildings clean, keep moving." He checked his watch, "Time for me to clean, OK sir?"

Kevin thanked him and handed him his card. "Call me if you hear anything suspicious. I appreciate your time." They shook hands.

Kevin sat back down to write up some notes in his pad, with a familiar unsettled feeling in his stomach. Time for lunch? *Follow your hunches.* From a previous case, he knew a guy in internal audit. He dialed him now. "Billy, do me a favor. Pull the last, say, six months of transactions signed off by Dory Johnson. Yeah, she's a building manager over on West Campus. Sort of a fishing expedition. Right, yeah, I get it - sounds fishy." He grunted an obligatory laugh. "Thanks, man."

Questioning the cleaning crew always dampened Kevin's state of mind. He felt some kinship with them – working-class people doing essential work for the university, wearing different uniforms, and similarly overlooked. And he meant literally overlooked - most of the students and faculty thoughtlessly scattered empty water bottles, candy wrappers and crumpled papers in their wake – the detritus of learning - while looking right past the cleaners and taking each morning's sparkling halls, pathways, and classrooms for granted. It was galling; Kevin tried not to dwell on it too much. The university offered great benefits and solid, reliable employment. Reinaldo and his crew were obviously proud of their work. That was worth a great deal, Kevin thought.

Bringing himself back to the present, he looked left and saw Jason still sitting right there, smoking beside him.

"Sorry, man," he said. "I'm a little preoccupied about a case I'm working on."

"No worries. What's it about?"

"Oh, you know, I can't really say. Part of the job."

"Sure, of course. Do you like it? Your job, I mean. I'm thinking of switching my major to criminal justice. Or maybe being a lawyer."

"What about math? Aren't you a math major?"

"Yeah, but I can't tell what will be best for my future." Jason looked forlorn, as if it were a decision he needed to make right away.

"You'll figure it out. They are all good choices." Kevin was the last person to offer advice; he decided to stick to what he knew. "My case is just a simple theft, nothing too exciting."

"Oh yeah, I bet there's a lot of that around here. It's like, you can't even put your sweatshirt down without someone walking off with it. And since they all say the same thing, you can never identify your property. The place should be called Clone U."

"You got it," said Kevin. Unconsciously, he opted to let Jason maintain his simple view of petty theft, stolen six-packs, and granola bars taken from the community kitchens in the dorms. Whatever new officer was sitting at the first desk in headquarters took these complaints all day long.

"I have a theory about it." Jason went on. "Lots of kids here…they go on and on about intangible stuff – philosophy, places they've been, the 'best' place for a fish taco, even a college education itself. They act like these intangible things are higher or more important than physical stuff. But I think that's because they've always had everything they really need. They don't understand how important stuff can be. Like, one time I went on this week-long hiking trip at camp, and it was cold out there. And I had this thermal shirt…it was magical. By the end of the trip, I loved that shirt. I felt like that shirt saved me. I still have it. There's a lot of privilege wrapped up in the attitude that physical things don't matter."

Kevin trained a hard look on Jason, thinking maybe he had underestimated him. Jason's words made him think about why he had been so uncomfortable talking with Reinaldo. Why he always felt wrong about questioning the cleaning crew. His mind jumped to a blue and white mixing bowl he had in his apartment. When he had moved his mother to Glenhurst, it was one of the few things he had held onto from the family house he grew up in. It reminded him of a hundred happy memories – making pancakes with his dad, a big bowl of popcorn watching movies together under a blanket on the couch, his mother mixing sugar cookies at the holidays. All these experiences long gone, but somehow invested in that blue and white bowl sitting on his kitchen shelf. His bowl was different from Jason's shirt though. The bowl didn't stand between him and frostbite; instead it reminded him of the fleetness of time and the people he missed.

"Do you think you love the shirt because it kept you warm back then, or because now it reminds you of the trip?"

"That's a great question, man. I'm gonna ponder that one. The trip was challenging, but it was also an adventure, so I do feel nostalgic about it. Even then, I was aware that it would become a great memory. And it was fucking freezing, so there was that." They exchanged rueful smiles as they dragged on their cigarettes. Jason continued, "Sometimes I think about refugees – people who leave some brutal situation with just the clothes on their backs. I imagine they are just trying to stay warm. They probably want to burn that stuff and kill those memories." They smoked in silence for a bit. "Still, I don't think people should steal stuff. No matter what, it's bad karma."

They heard the instructor's voice, calling them back from break.

As they stood to go, stubbing out their cigarettes and stretching, Kevin said, "Well, bad karma is pretty much what keeps me in business. And that really is something to ponder."

Chapter 5 – Sheila

      Kevin arrived 10 minutes early, thinking his date might appreciate not having to wait alone for him by the door. He watched as the other customers filed in for the Thursday night, 8:00 p.m. painting class at the Art Barn. Two cheerful young women were running the place. One oversaw the bar and the other apparently was the instructor.

      The vibe was friendly and loud, a one-eighty from what he experienced in night school at the university. The room was laid out like a normal classroom, with two rows of long tables facing a wide, low dais in front. On the dais was an easel and a small table holding a jar of water, a second jar of brushes, and a few clean rags. At each student chair, there was a similar set of tools alongside a small tabletop easel and a perfectly clean, white canvas. Upbeat music streamed from hidden speakers, almost as if they were about to start a spin class at the gym.

      A big family group walked in together. The man went straight for the beer while the woman, two kids, and grandmother noisily debated how to choose the best seats. They settled in the front row, right in front of where the instructor would be standing. The wife dropped her purse and followed her husband to the bar. The two kids rolled their eyes at each other, then one started idly chewing a strand of her hair while the other pulled his phone from his jeans and went blank-faced staring into its depths. The grandma busied herself sorting Kleenex among the many zippered compartments in her black bag.

Behind them, a twenty-something Asian couple walked in, hesitating about where to sit. Kevin wondered if the guy had lost a bet or something, but he was also reassured by the date-like vibe they were giving off. They exchanged tight-lipped smiling grimaces and sat in the back row.

And then a bachelorette party arrived, all chirps and whoops, cold air and loud heels. When did bachelorettes become such a thing? Oh man. The immediate vicinity of the campus was usually safe from this element – but the Art Barn was outside the perimeter. From their flushed cheeks and loud voices, he suspected they had been pre-gaming. Sure enough, there was a pink party van illegally parked by the curb outside. The driver sat inside in a hazy neon glow. Kevin decided to step outside for a cigarette to let the noise settle down.

No sooner had he cleared the door and lit up when one of the women followed him back outside.

"Kevin?"

It was her. Sheila. Not wanting to stare at the bachelorettes, he had missed her coming in behind them. She was shorter than her profile picture suggested and wider and she wore glasses. She was probably thinking the same thing about him: people always looked better in photos. They shook hands, and he recognized the smile that had attracted his attention in the first place. He offered her a cigarette.

"No thanks, I don't smoke." Damn. Of course, he had seen that on her profile but had nervously forgotten.

"Let me put this out," he offered.

"No, no need. Enjoy it. The smell makes me nostalgic." Her face looked like she meant it, so Kevin shrugged and continued.

"You work at the university?" He nodded, inhaling.

"What do you teach?"

This was an occupational hazard of working at the university. Everyone always asked that, and then looked puzzled when you explained that you were not a member of the faculty. It's like, no one expects every single person in a hospital to be a doctor, right? Why are colleges different? But it never failed. He tried not to hold it against her. He said he was a campus detective.

"Detective? Like, doing investigations? Like, people cheating on exams and stuff?" He sighed and explained that the university community was bigger than many small cities, and the whole range of people passed through — students and teachers, but also chefs, janitors, bus drivers, accountants, nurses, engineers, crooks, thieves…all walks of life. It always bugged him to have to explain that, but it was uncanny. People really did not think about it. He felt his energy waning. He dragged on his butt, trying to formulate a follow-up question.

She smiled tentatively and said, "Huh. That makes total sense; I never thought about it."

"How about you? You work in software development?" He realized by asking that he knew as little about that as she knew about police work.

"Yes, I do in-house app development for a financial services firm. Pretty exciting, right?"

"That question is way out of my league," Kevin replied with a grin.

"Well, I guess I'll go in and save us a couple of seats. Away from the bachelorettes, if possible." Score one for her. As soon as she turned away, he dropped the cigarette and headed back in. He stopped at the bar, calling over to ask her what she would like to drink. He bought cups of beer and wine and brought them over to the seats she had selected.

His red solo cup of beer was identical to the cup of rinse water.

"I'll have to be careful not to mix these up," he observed.

Sheila laughed, "I think you would notice right away."

The instructor called the class to order, her manner patronizing them like preschoolers.

"OK. Don't be intimidated by painting! This is a judgment free zone – and you are especially not allowed to judge *your own work* harshly. We are here to *have fun*. You have four brushes. We are going to call them Big Brush (she waved around the largest brush) – yes, everyone hold it up! And this one is Flat Brush (waving), Round Brush (waving), and this one, my favorite, is Baby Brush. And we say that in a little teeny voice, like this... *Beeby Bwush*. Everyone say it with me."

Sheila sipped her wine and gave him a sidelong glance. "Hang in there..." she said. "I think her day job might be teaching kindergarten."

It really wasn't so bad. Once they got started, the instructor turned the music up loud so they didn't have to hear any bachelorette hijinks – they could still talk a bit but not be overheard by the people around them. Kevin always thought it was relaxing to put brushstrokes on a surface, even if the setting was scripted and, yes, definitely cheesy. They were painting a snowy landscape, with moonlight on a frozen pond and little brightly colored figures ice skating. It was carefully composed, and Kevin enjoyed executing the sections, step by step, while watching Sheila out of the corner of his eye. He liked the way she held her brush, and the intensity of her concentration. She looked happy – engaged but not nervous, and not blowing it off either. She didn't seem self-conscious about her painting, or about the situation itself. She was just...calm. He admired her nonchalance and tried to mirror it back to her. He relaxed into the scene – the beer, the brushstrokes, and the fact that Sheila was clearly enjoying herself.

"I can imagine software development being exciting…" he ventured.

"I guess. It pays the bills but my real thing is art. I love drawing, building, sculpting. I wanted to come here because I thought I might make a few bucks teaching this stuff. I have my own kit at the maker space over in Stilton…you know the one?"

He didn't really, so he asked, "What's a maker space?"

"It's like a big warehouse building full of little cubbies where different artists keep their tools – you know, like looms and power tools and 3D printers, and machining equipment. And you can borrow other people's tools, which is great, and learn how to use them, and go to classes on different stuff, like 'Make a Birdhouse' or whatever, and you can offer classes in the stuff you know how to do. It's just this totally rad thing. I could show you sometime. Being there really sparks my creativity."

"And it's just artists?" Kevin wondered how did he not know about this? It was the kind of quirky thing that tended to crop up in a university town, and he loved that stuff.

"Not all; some are artists, some are making prototypes for start-ups, some are artisans who sell their stuff at farmers markets and such. Like the guy next to me works leather. He makes bags and belts. He's trying to learn how to make shoes, but that turns out to be a very technical thing!"

"I never thought about it. What do you make?"

"I make all kinds of stuff, but my obsession is hand-painting designs on everything."

Looking at her canvas, Kevin noticed that she had begun to stray from the instructions. Large sections were starting to flip colors – as if she had a mental color wheel and was intentionally choosing the most opposite color.

When the instructor talked about the deep blue of the sky, Sheila made it orange. The white snow was red. Her moon was purple. It was a strangely arresting image…like his own, but opposite. He kept glancing over, intrigued, even as his own painting took shape in the more standard way.

"Right now," she said, continuing to paint, "I'm making this enormous sculpture out of found objects, metal and wood and fabric and glass. I can't wait to paint it. It's taking up my whole section. I noticed some stuff near the dumpsters here when I parked the car… I may need to check them out for good stuff before we leave tonight."

"Can I help? Maybe you'll need help carrying something. Sounds interesting." She was different. Kevin was more than curious and wanted her to see him as someone who could match her, impulse for impulse, not playing by the rules.

"Sure. We could investigate together." She winked at him.

The soundtrack was blaring that song about wanting to swing from the chandelier. Kevin got up to get a second round of drinks. They turned back to their paintings.

"OK, class. The final step is snowflakes!" Kevin realized that the snowflakes in the model painting had been ever-so-slightly stressing him out all night. So small, so precise, and any false move would smear the whole sky. Not his forte at all. The instructor continued, "Take your *Beeby Bwush* (tipsy laughter from the bachelorettes), turn it around and dip the handle tip into your white paint. Now just touch that tip to the canvas…" It was so simple, a trick he would never have thought of. Kevin felt a simple joy flow through his bloodstream, no doubt following the path blazed by the beers he had drunk. This was what he loved about art –the combination of creating something where there had been nothing before, informed by learning technical solutions, which you could practice and improve, and see your work transformed.

Sheila said, "Hey." He realized he had been totally absorbed in the silly snowflake work.

"You are smiling at your canvas!" She looked delighted, which made him happy. "Hold still," she said and reached over with her brush tip and gently touched his cheek. "You are really into those snowflakes!" she said.

He could feel the dot of paint stiffen on his skin as it began to dry and resisted the urge to wipe it off. He thought it would be too much to poke her back. Instead he just smiled.

"I guess I am a big flake."

She laughed, and he felt it echo in his chest along with the paint, the music, and the beer. She's fun, he thought. This is fun. We need to do this again. Follow your hunches; don't rush things.

When the class was over, he walked her to her car. As promised, she took a quick detour to the dumpster where they found a few broken pine pallets leaning against the outside. He helped her load them into the hatch of her Subaru.

She pulled a flashlight from the trunk, saying, "OK with you if I check inside the dumpster? I'll need a boost to be able to see over the edge." Kevin laced his fingers together, and she put a steadying hand on his shoulder as she stepped into his hand cradle. She was lighter than he expected.

Shining her flashlight around the interior, she reported it empty, then said, "Actually, I'm kind of relieved. I don't really want to end a first date by climbing into a dumpster…but I wouldn't be able to resist if there was treasure in there." He had been wondering about the same thing…did she really plan to jump in, and was he ready to follow? He thought, yeah, he probably was.

"What would have qualified as treasure?" he asked.

"Ah, such a great question. I never know it until I see it." He could hear the broad smile in her voice, even though the lights in the parking lot were dim. He walked her to her car, where she forthrightly stuck out her hand and said, "This was fun. I hope we can do it again." Her smile was encouraging, and he replied, "For sure! I'll call you soon."

Walking into his condo afterward, he tossed his keys on the counter and pulled a beer out of the fridge. It was a local IPA, much better than the cheap drinks at the Art Barn. He sat down at his computer and googled "maker space Stilton." There it was – a well-designed website with a great photo gallery of random equipment, art works, and events. There was a shot of two guys racing bicycles around a miniature banked velodrome made of plywood. They looked like they were probably insane, but he admired their commitment. He clicked on Classes. Figure drawing, watercolor and ceramics but also chainmail, cosplay, and near the bottom 'Make your own sex toys.' And right next to that, a picture of Sheila surrounded by observers, wearing safety goggles as she demonstrated how to solder the wiring inside what was unequivocally a large pink dildo. Kevin said out loud in the empty room, "Whoa." He leaned back in his chair, eyes wide. He took a swig of beer to mask his discomfort from himself. That old song *Superfreak* started playing in his head.

When dealing with emotional shocks, Kevin's reaction times tended to be slow. He always told himself that it was possible, and even adaptive, for his emotional response time to be temperate and measured, even while his physical response to danger was fast and alert. He made a clear distinction between the two and didn't trust those moments when his feelings shot out ahead. It was a bit like having a poker face. Better to step back from the situation and let it sink in. Come back to it later. This worked on the job, where keeping other people calm was often the first priority.

Alone in his apartment, as he rose calmly from his chair and rinsed his empty beer bottle in the sink, his subconscious mind was already processing the fact that he didn't really know her that well, that it was a free country, and that he could acknowledge artistic expression was a spectrum. He placed the bottle carefully in the recycling bin, then flopped onto the couch, and clicked the TV remote to show SportsCenter, so he could catch up on the day's scores. But underneath his impassive face and radiating back from his outstretched arm as he pointed the remote at the screen, his mind was chewing worriedly on the image of Sheila teaching a roomful of obedient students how to make sex toys. He remembered how calm she seemed and wondered how sexually confident a person must be to teach a class like that. What else was she into? He played back the unconventional choices she had made, even in the controlled environment of the art class. The color reversals, the dumpster diving. He wondered if, taken together, it was just all too much. Was she too much; maybe her personality was bigger than he was looking for? Was this a red flag that he had missed in his initial perusal of Hinge profiles?

Kevin's thoughts immediately went to Heather, his last real girlfriend. In his mind's eye, she shook her head in disappointment. *Dude, the red flag is you, not her.* He would let it go. Stop looking for flaws. Take it one step at a time. Looking back at the evening, he remembered that her difference had pleased him. When he agreed that it had been a great, fun evening, he meant it.

On the screen, two deskbound sports pundits argued with overplayed intensity about a long, looping basketball shot from an earlier game, replaying the same two second clip backward and forward six times. Was it three points? Was his toe on the line? Kevin let the artificial conflict on the screen distract him from his own thoughts.

A bit later, walking into his bathroom to brush his teeth before bed, something about his reflection in the shaving mirror stopped him. Leaning in, he saw the dot of black paint on his cheek. It took him a minute to remember what it was…and why the dot wasn't white. It was supposed to be snow, after all. He stretched his jaw and rubbed away the paint, with *superfreak, superfreak, she's super freaky* pounding away repeatedly in his brain. He soothed himself to sleep with the knowledge that he didn't need to make this decision tonight. They had a good time. He had broken the ice and gone on a date. He didn't need to let his thoughts race ahead.

Chapter 6 – Homecoming

In CAMPO, everybody worked homecoming –
case or no case, motion sensor or no motion sensor. And
these days, it was a serious gig.

Everyone in the country had heard the frightening
news accounts of campus disasters – natural, accidental,
and terroristic. No one took things lightly anymore. For
the past few years, the university had been running crisis
management tabletop exercises to train for things going
horribly wrong during the big events like homecoming,
commencement, and alumni reunions. These training
events included anyone who might be onsite, role-playing
scenarios that ranged from medical emergencies to bomb
threats and active shooters. You would show up for the
training with no preparation and immediately be plunged
into something that looked like the climax of a zombie
apocalypse. Kevin remembered one year, the facilities guy
sitting next to him leaned over and said, "This happens,
I'm in my truck headed for the Texas hill country." He had
to admit there was some wisdom to the guy's perspective.

Homecoming wasn't about pranks and rivalries
anymore. The state cops were routinely on hand. This year
there were a couple of VIP politicos from Washington in
the president's box, so the local FBI outfit had sent out
three plainclothes guys with earpieces. Of course, the VIPs
had their own security details too. Kevin was glad that
coordinating all the levels of security was Mulally's
problem. Better him than me, he thought.

It was mid-morning and so far, things were going smoothly. Kevin had requested the assignment guarding the major donor tent, which had a place of honor near the football stadium. His job was to hover unobtrusively near the entrance, nodding reassuringly behind dark glasses as people passed through the opening, which was garlanded with bunting, ivy and golden blossoms. Inside the tent, there was a fake floor like a putting green in case of mud, enough flowers to give the place a faint whiff of mortuary, and silver champagne flutes embossed with the university crest. Bartenders in crisp white shirts kept the booze flowing, even at eleven am. The football game was scheduled for one o'clock, so the crowd was not yet at its peak. Outside, there was bright sun and unseasonably hot weather, with no shade in the acres-wide athletic quad. In full uniform, Kevin could feel the sweat starting under his collar and dripping all the way down to where it soaked the back of his waistband. He was squinting behind his sunglasses, trying to look alert but also keep a low profile. Part of the gig at an event like this was to recede into the background. The idea was to engender goodwill and generosity by invisibly making everyone feel safe and relaxed. Standing there in full police regalia, his job felt like equal parts public safety and performance art.

People were having a good time. Every year, a couple of guys showed up in raccoon coats and straw boaters, looking to recreate some imaginary ideal of collegiate spirit they'd seen in history books. About half the men in the tent wore heavy class rings; the same number of women wore scarves or cardigans in the official goldenrod and green school colors. The women looked to be half the age of the men, which Kevin attributed to a combination of hair dye, second marriages, and generally just trying harder. Not for the first time, Kevin marveled at the incredible tribal rhythm that pulsed through the crowd.

It had been about a week since his date with Sheila. He hadn't called her, even though he knew the clock was ticking. She hadn't called him either. Each day he thought, "I liked her; what's the big deal," but then he didn't pick up the phone. He asked himself if he was intimidated, and he wasn't sure. Was she the confident, open person she had appeared to be, or was her dildo class an obvious red flag that she was some kind of sexual psycho? He actively tamped down the temptation to do some background checking. Instead, he just kept ruminating on the situation and procrastinating.

And now his trained eye was drawn toward three people slowly approaching his spot. Eureka. One of the three was Marie-Claude Aprille from the fund-raising team. He had requested this assignment hoping she might be around, and he watched her closely as she guided an elderly couple forward, gracefully gesturing as she described the new addition to the field house across the lawn. She nodded at Kevin in a friendly way, and his gaze followed as the three made their way into the cool dimness of the tent. As she entered, she pushed her sunglasses up onto her head with a flick of her hair, a gesture that struck him as achingly sexy. Marie-Claude was originally from Jamaica. Kevin had met her a few times around campus; she was gorgeous and her accent slayed him.

Her charges safely delivered to the ministrations of the bartenders, she turned and headed back in his direction, with a little crease between her brows. She walked like a dancer, purposeful but not hurried.

"Detective Conley, right? We met at the provost's dinner last spring. I'm Marie-Claude," she said.

Kevin stuck out his hand to shake. "Yes, nice to see you again. Everything OK?" It was too much to hope that there was some small thing he could do for her.

"Oh yes, of course, but I do need your help with something. It's not urgent, but before you leave today, be a dear and walk over to Gate C. There's a new granite bench just outside the gate that I want you to check out. It's another hoax, and we really need to get to the bottom of it."

"Hoax?" Kevin didn't understand how a bench could be a hoax. Would it collapse under an overweight member of the Class of '92?

"Right, it has a gift inscription on it, but it's not real. Someone just had it made and plonked it down, no university gift attached."

"Why would someone do that? A granite bench probably cost a few thou."

"Right, and that's a lot less money than a donor bench. Crazy as it sounds, we've had three recent incidents like this. Not a life/safety concern," Kevin noted her use of the crisis tabletop lingo, "but please do check it out while you're here and let's talk next week. How am I supposed to cultivate donors when people just go around decorating the campus on their own, all ray ray?" She smiled a tight little smile and headed back into the tent, smoothing her skirt and delicately blotting a bead of perspiration from her temple with a golden cocktail napkin. Kevin shivered in the heat, as another line of sweat goosebumped down his spine.

Ray ray. Who talks like that? The possibility of working on her case, no matter how trivial it sounded, kept his spirits up and thoughts of Sheila at bay through the rest of the long hot day. Marie-Claude passed his post several more times over the course of the afternoon, and each time he nodded and tried to look like the strong, capable man you would want to solve your big problems.

First thing on Monday, after grabbing coffee from Starbucks, Kevin sat at his desk looking at three pictures of hoaxes. He had snapped a shot of the Gate C bench; Marie Claude had emailed photos of the other two. He printed out all three and laid them side by side on his desk. The first one was a simple granite cube, about the size of a hibachi. It had been placed near a bike rack at the law school; no one knew exactly when. The Law Dean had taken up commuting to school on his bike a few months ago, and when he tripped over it while trying to unlock his Trek one afternoon, he sent an angry note to the University Development Office. The inscription read "Hale Fellows." There was no record of the gift – and the development office prided itself on being circumspect in acknowledging and tracking philanthropic contributions. Kevin had just learned there was a person whose sole job was to do just that – she was called The Recording Secretary, and all she did, literally, was record gifts. He wondered how a person got a job like that. Anyway, Buildings & Grounds dug up the granite hibachi, replaced the sod, and put it in storage over at the Shuttle Bus depot.

The second one, which had also ended up with the shuttle buses, was discovered by the groundskeepers when they were out raking last fall. It had been nestled between a couple of yews just inside the perimeter fence of the main quad. It was an obelisk, a two-foot-tall Washington Monument, inscribed with the word "Scruffy," written top to bottom. Again, there was no record of a gift. When he asked Marie Claude about it, she acted like her professionalism had been challenged.

"Do you really think we would turn the campus into a pet cemetery? Scruffy, really. Seriously, you would not believe some of the requests we get – and we try to spin them into gold." They both smiled at the reference.

"It isn't easy to take someone who wants to leave his aunt's denture collection to the medical school and ever-so-gently persuade him that a $100,000 contribution to the scholarship fund would be a more fitting tribute to dear Aunt Edna," she continued. Kevin was starting to appreciate the challenge of MC's job.

The homecoming hoax was more ambitious. It was a simple bench, made of three pieces of granite – two upright supports and a wide, beautifully polished seat. On the front edge of the seat, there was an inscription.

Beautiful Lucy Smithers, the Class of '83 loved you well.

Kevin was considering all the possible interpretations – was she a vivacious classmate? Beloved instructor? Cook in a frat? Free love hippy? Was it the whole class, or just a few? And what exactly did they mean by "well." He sensed someone looking over his shoulder. Maybe it was the loud breathing. Mulally.

"Is this one of your art projects, Conley?"

"Hey chief. I'm investigating fraudulent donor memorials, at the request of the development office. This bench appeared mysteriously at Homecoming. It's the damnedest thing. Some people don't have enough to do."

"Huh. Well, good news," Mulally said, slapping a small oval device on his desk. "The motion sensor in Waverly is officially activated. Here's the beeper. Carry it with you; it will buzz if anything trips the signal in 12C."

Kevin grabbed for the device, about the size of a sporty car fob with a similar silver ring loop. It was smooth to the touch and would fit easily in his pocket.

"Nice. I'll keep it with me all day."

"Right. Look, this is key: we're only authorized to enter during normal business hours for now. Nothing heroic. No more stakeouts."

Kevin nodded. It didn't make much sense to him, but he figured he'd scored a win and didn't want to push it. Mulally looked back at the blurry photos spread on his desk.

"So this week, looks like your beat is crazy alums. Here's another one for you." Mulally dropped a large Ziploc bag on the desk. It looked like sand but landed with a clunk. "Somebody is spreading ashes under the trees again…"

"Oh, for fuck's sake."

"I know; it freaks out the grounds crew. If it was just ashes, that would be one thing. The problem is the little bits of bone. We have to check it out. Go take a look on the west side of the music building."

"There's never enough evidence to solve these things…"

"I know, but we have to show some interest. Bring over a couple of baggies and a trowel, in case you find any more, ah, evidence." His left eyebrow rose a notch with the word evidence, but the rest of his face remained impassive.

"And make sure you open a case file on the fake donor whatsis." Mulally tapped on Kevin's desk and shuffled back to his office.

Kevin sighed, grabbing his hat and pad on the way out. These ash spreaders were a real nuisance, maybe even a public health risk. It happened a few times each year, and Kevin could just imagine how clever the bereaved families thought they were being, sneaking on campus in the dark of night to fulfill dear old dad's last wish. He could picture the conversations around kitchen tables across the state. Some would be like, "Yeah, it's the only way he's ever getting in there, har har" and others would be like, "They wanted us to consider planned giving, well here it is, har har." Each family thought they had a unique and outrageous idea. It was a miracle they didn't trip over each other under the bushes as they dumped out their urns. Again with the identity mingling. Kevin really could not fathom how they could love a bunch of buildings so much that they wanted to spend eternity under the foundation plantings. A couple of years earlier, CAMPO had considered running a DNA check on a particularly egregious sample. But, with the DNA testing cost topping out at fifteen hundred dollars, and of course the strong possibility of pissing off highly engaged donors, the cost/benefit just didn't add up.

Thinking of eternity made him realize he hadn't visited his mother in a couple weeks. He should really do that. And should he just go ahead and call Sheila already?

Pulling on gloves, he made the rounds of the music building, dropping to his hands and knees to bag any suspicious-looking material. After a quick sweep, he rested on a bench, red from the sun and the exertion, not to mention the mild humiliation of skulking in the bushes like some kind of pervert. He would have been better off undercover, outfitted as a gardener. After a cigarette, he pulled out his pad to sketch the elaborate cornice jutting from the corner of the music building. Looking closely, he noticed that each cornice was slightly different, and had the name of a famous composer engraved into it. It reminded him of the phony monuments. Was there some theme that unified the hoaxes, like the cornices, or was it more like the human remains, just a bunch of random nut jobs with the same lack of originality. At least the latest one had a name attached. What could he learn about the beloved Miss Smithers? Marie-Claude might be able to help track her down in the alumni database. Intriguing, but first he had to log in this random bag of grey powder, possibly human remains, tag the plastic bag, and lock it into the glorified supply closet they referred to at CAMPO headquarters as the evidence room. He sighed and returned to the office.

Back at his desk, he discovered that his email was lit up with new messages. Six different faculty members and three administrators had each forwarded notes from one Priscilla Sturgis. Jesus, it had been almost a year since he'd seen her name. She must be off her meds again. He remembered his father saying that when it comes to police work, "crazy comes in threes." They should never schedule homecoming during a full moon. He refilled his coffee mug and settled in to scan the latest volley.

Ms. Sturgis had been a research fellow at the Institute for International Affairs for a few months, almost five years ago. Kevin had never met her, but that wasn't unusual. It was after she completed her fellowship and left that something seemed to go haywire. First there were complaints: computer spyware, environmental allergic reactions, identity theft – these came to the administrators at the Institute. They tried to brush her off with polite noncommittal sympathy – after all, she was gone so there wasn't much they could do. Then she started contacting the faculty with increasingly weird claims. To the female faculty, she complained of sexual harassment from the men. In fact, that was the first time Kevin had become aware of Fensbridge – he was one of the people she fingered for harassment, and just as Kevin was about to launch a formal investigation, the rest of the complaints came flying in. To the male faculty, including Fensbridge himself, she spun tales of competitive women colleagues stealing her ideas and her data out of jealousy. At the height of it, several complaints landed on his desk simultaneously, as one by one people got spooked by the volume and intensity of her rants.

Even with a superficial investigation, it was clear that there was a mental health component to her situation, so Kevin contacted the university's mental health professionals, who quietly discovered that she had been admitted to a mental hospital downstate. He never heard the details because of privacy law, but after conferring with the general counsel, they had decided her concerns were likely unfounded and they sent her a politely worded request to desist from sending emails. Kevin was the designated point person, charged with consolidating and monitoring her communications going forward. It was sad, but no action need be taken unless the intensity rose again.

He glanced through the messages quickly and was relieved to discover there was nothing newly threatening or alarming in them. He thanked the various sources for forwarding them along and filed the whole batch into the special folder he had created for her.

Next on the docket was to google the names associated with the fake monuments: Hale, Scruffy, Lucy Smithers. Not for the first time that day, he reflected that this was not what he had expected back at the police academy. He reached into his pocket to check the motion detector beeper – maybe there was some real police work that needed attention. The device was silent as a stone. Kevin slapped it against his palm, wondering if it was dead, but the battery light flickered and steadied. He opened his left desk drawer to toss it in and noticed an unopened pack of Twizzlers in there. Ah, sustenance. This was just what he needed to power through the tedious and probably hopeless task of online searching. It was also a reminder to visit his mother, so he made a mental note. Maybe Wednesday.

He decided to start with the university database, to narrow the field. Half a sticky bag later, Kevin hit pay dirt and bolted upright in his chair. According to the class notes from the class of 1983, published in 1988, one Howard Finkelstein had married a Miss Lucy Smithers in Hot Springs, Arkansas in 1986 and was soon the proud papa of promising athlete Josh Finkelstein. Flushed with excitement, he reached for his phone to call Marie-Claude.

"Marie-Claude, do you know an alum named Finkelstein, class of 1983?"

"The name doesn't ring a bell," she said, "But I only deal with the high-capacity donors." Kevin wondered to himself who came up with these euphemisms. He would have just called them Millionaires. He could hear her tapping at her keyboard in the background. "Yes, here he is. Gives about $25 a year, but only when someone calls. Hardly worth the time, really. Why do you ask?"

"I'm researching the fake bench. He married Lucy Smithers, the lady whose name is on the bench."

"Ah, beautiful. So we call him up and pounce?" Together they figured out a plan, based on the idea that it would be better for Finkelstein to hear from the development office than the campus police. They would make the call from Marie-Claude's office, tomorrow at two. Kevin would take special care shaving. Well, that wasn't part of the official plan; he kept that to himself.

Twenty-four hours later, facing each other across Marie-Claude's tidy desk, they were both dumbstruck. The call had not gone as expected. Marie-Claude reached for a Kleenex, and gingerly wiped the corner of her eye as she took a shaky breath. Kevin didn't know what to say.

They had reached Howard Finkelstein with no trouble – he picked up on the third ring. When Marie-Claude introduced herself, he had jumped right in.

"I'm not going to be able to contribute this year; I'm sorry. Things are tight."

Marie-Claude smiled at Kevin.

"Oh no trouble at all, you've been very generous. We're calling about another matter. I'm here with my colleague Kevin Conley, to inquire about a monument that was recently placed on campus."

Kevin started to tell him about the bench, but as soon as he mentioned the inscription, Howard Finkelstein burst into noisy, wet-sounding tears. He kept talking, but they couldn't make out everything he said.

"Oh no. (sob) She's gone! Lucy is dead, we were married for 35 years. (nose blowing) She died 2 weeks ago. She wasn't even sick; she just keeled over; the doctors say it was an aneurism. I don't know what to do. A monument? I don't know what you're talking about. It doesn't make any sense."

Marie-Claude tried to recover, saying she was sorry for his loss, but her words couldn't dam the flood of his grief.

"She was so young, barely 60. We were planning a walking tour of the Ozarks this summer. (sniffle) She's gone. I haven't been alone for 35 years. And Josh is so busy and so far away. I tried to go back to work, but I just break down every time I see her photo on my desk. She was the most beautiful girl I ever saw." They looked guiltily at each other as Howard Finkelstein loudly blew his nose.

Kevin broke in again with condolences, and offered to call at a better time, but Howard cut him off.

"No, no I'm glad you called. Sorry I'm such a basket case. A monument on the campus? There must be some kind of mistake. Lucy wasn't even a student – she was a local girl. She worked in the grocery store – that's how we met. She had other friends there, though. Some of them still send Christmas cards. Oh my god, I just realized I need to let those people know. Hollingsworth and Shipley and the Joneses. Everybody loved Lucy."

Marie-Claude finally eased him off the line, making a note on her pad to send a sympathy card from the university. They sat in silence for a minute or two.

"Holy cow," said Kevin.

"Indeed," said Marie-Claude.

Kevin glanced down at his own pad and saw the names he'd scribbled. Hollingsworth. Shipley. Jones. He asked her if any of the names were familiar.

With a little sigh and a shake of her head, Marie-Claude turned to her computer screen. "Yes," she said, typing. Hollingsworth is one of ours." She squinted into the blue light, the little crease appearing on her forehead. "Roger Hollingsworth, Class of '83. Wall Street guy. He gives $10,000 every year. He was at homecoming. Twice married; five kids all told. Three of the kids are also alums: Roger Junior '06, Randall '08, and Rebecca, Class of '10."

"He could be a lead," suggested Kevin. "He could even be the guy."

The crease in her forehead deepened. "Well, that's a whole other matter, isn't it. I need to think about this. I mean, he's given us almost a half million dollars, not counting the tuition he's paid. I need to tread lightly."

"Let's try Shipley, looking in the class of '83. Jones is too common a name."

They found Shipley, again in the class notes. He was an attorney in the Manhattan DA's office, a long-time public servant. They called him together; Kevin decided to take the lead this time, on the logic that it was one law and order guy to another. By referring to himself as Detective Conley, he succeeded in getting through to Shipley's direct line.

Using the speakerphone, Kevin introduced Shipley and Marie-Claude. He ran through the basic description of the bench and stated that it was of unknown provenance. He asked if Mr. Shipley might know anything about it and was met by an awkwardly long pause on the other end of the line.

"Mr. Shipley? Are you still there?"

"And why are you calling me about this, exactly?"

"Well, Mr. Finkelstein mentioned you, Hollingsworth and Jones as other friends of Ms. Smithers. So we are just following up."

They heard a snort on the line; there was something dark in the sound.

"Reuben Jones? Friends...huh. And you plan to call Hollingsworth as well?"

"Yes, sir, we do."

"Well, I can't help you with this. I wish you luck." The line went dead.

And that was it. Kevin's gut told him that Shipley knew more than he was letting on, but also that as a lawyer, he wasn't likely to say much more. At least they now had a full name on Jones. Given that this was more a prank than a crime, he might have been willing to let it go. But there was Marie-Claude, sitting across from him, her eyes lit up.

"Well, this is just getting more and more interesting! Is this what your job is always like, doing investigations and solving mysteries...what fun! Maybe we should make one of those cork boards with suspects and clues, pushpins and strings connecting them all...like in *Castle*."

That was all the cajoling it took to persuade Kevin to give Reuben Jones a call – Marie-Claude was still trying to avoid Hollingsworth if possible. And since this was the real world, Jones was traveling and unavailable. They made an appointment to call him the following week, and when she hung up the phone, Kevin sagged at the disappointment he saw in MC's eyes. Trying to sound like a TV detective, he told her to buck up. "Patience is a big part of investigative work. Never give up/never rush it."

Walking back to HQ, he scanned the messages on his phone. Three more messages from Ms. Sturgis, including a forwarded email from Fensbridge with a cc. to Mulally, with the header, "Can't you people make this harassment stop?" Shit. He would have to deal with that one. He also saw the regular notification from Glenhurst. There was no news; just a pro forma message that his family member would love to see him. That always gave him a gut punch of guilt, mostly because he knew that he needed those reminders to do the right thing. Today, feeling the wave of adrenaline that accompanied investigative progress, Kevin decided to channel it down the road to Glenhurst. He was feeling strong.

That evening, he swung left during his commute and headed out to visit his mother. He parked, changed his jacket, and rearranged his face into a smile as he prepared to repeat the usual routine. When he knocked on the door to her room, Mary turned slowly in her chair. "What seems to be the trouble, Officer?"

Kevin sat on the edge of the bed and made small talk, gently correcting her when her responses revealed the gaps and jumps in her memory. Mostly she was silent though, which made it both easier and harder. He sketched as he sat. After twenty minutes or so, Kevin put his pad away and got up.

"Well, Mom, I need to hit the road. It's great to see you."

"Good to see you, Officer. If you see my husband, tell him he should come visit. He hasn't been here since yesterday."

Kevin swallowed hard. "I will, ma'am. I'll do that. You take care." Depleted, Kevin retreated down the long hallway toward the glowing exit sign.

If your own mother doesn't recognize you, who are you? As he walked along the deserted, dim corridor, Kevin felt very alone. Maybe that was the source of all this intensity over homecoming – and all these silly-ass fake memorials – maybe that's what it was all about. This was their tribe. Kevin might think it was idiotic and false, but that didn't stop him, deep down, from envying the connection they felt. Kevin wasn't sure he felt that connected to anything; since his father's death he sometimes thought he was just free-floating, adrift in the world. And his mother, she had lost it all, staring out the window. She barely knew who she was, and yet still she kept clinging to life.

He tossed tonight's drawing into the trunk, then walked around and dropped into the driver's seat, closing his eyes and taking a few deep, steadying breaths. As he started the car and turned toward his address, the monuments remained on his mind. No wonder people want to plonk down some granite and tether themselves to reality, or at least to a version of reality that they like. *Scruffy*, for god's sake. As Kevin drove out of the parking lot, he idly wondered if maybe he should get a dog. Do pets get dementia? Or will your dog always love you? To cheer himself, Kevin thought aloud, "I could definitely come up with a better name than Scruffy."

Chapter 7 – Resolution of the Fake Monuments Case

The next morning found Kevin back at his desk, nursing a Starbucks and trying to puzzle through the data and next steps on each of his three active cases: the fake monuments, the vacant apartment, and the uptick in threatening emails from the alumna. He pulled a sheet of paper from the recycling bin and turned it to the clean side. He flipped it to the landscape orientation and used a pencil stub to sketch out three columns. He labeled each column with a picture: a framed picture, a bench, and a cartoon woman's face with squiggly symbols coming from her head. In each column, he wrote down the big questions, and then an arrow to what he planned to do next to answer the question. For the vacant apartment, he was still in a waiting game: waiting for the motion sensor to buzz, waiting for the financial records to appear. On the threatening emails, he would call his contact in the general counsel's office – just in case they might interpret the latest activity differently than he had. He also needed to follow up with Fensbridge on the emails, and wondered if some subtle questioning there might serve a double purpose, revealing clues about what was going on in the vacant apartment. It was rare for two cases to overlap like that.

And of course, the call to Reuben Jones was scheduled for later that morning. Kevin checked his watch to make sure he wasn't already late. Seeing Mulally shambling toward his desk on the way to the coffee pot, Kevin shoved his worksheet under another file and turned his attention to the computer screen, where he busily mimicked typing up progress notes.

"Any progress on that bench?" Mulally asked, his cocked eyebrow and few words clearly communicating that he was humoring Kevin in the whole thing. Kevin brought him up to date and mentioned his appointment at the development office later that morning.

"She's very pretty, that fundraiser gal," said Mulally, as he poured sludge from the carafe into his stained mug.

"I guess," said Kevin, eyes glued to his screen. "I think we should be able to wrap up the case in a day or two." Mulally headed back to his office, tapping two quick knocks on Kevin's desk as he passed. Feeling sheepish, Kevin took a moment to persuade himself that his interest in Marie-Claude was not clouding his judgment. He checked his watch again.

Reuben Jones kept them waiting, but finally picked up the receiver. Through the speakerphone, he sounded harried and impatient; the voice of a man made irritable by life's unceasing demands. Marie-Claude introduced herself and described Kevin simply as "my colleague." She got straight to the point, asking him directly whether he had seen the bench dedicated to Lucy Smithers at the recent homecoming game.

Jones responded to the question with no hesitation. "Yeah, I saw it. Hollingsworth made a big point of showing it to me. Kind of childish – a prank really. Why are you calling *me* about it?"

Marie-Claude started to explain the university's guidelines about gifts and memorials and mentioned in passing that Lucy Smithers had died recently. Jones interrupted her.

"Wait a minute. You're saying that Lucy Smithers is dead?" They told him, quite generally, the circumstances of her death. After a long pause, he said, "Give me five minutes. I'm going to call you back." He hung up abruptly, leaving them staring at each other in surprise.

"Once again, this is getting very interesting," said Marie-Claude.

Kevin nodded, trying to work up the nerve to ask if she had lunch plans. Before he could speak, the phone rang again.

Jones' voice sounded entirely different this time – maybe it was the connection, or maybe it was something else. "Look. I'm going to level with you – and maybe it will help explain this dumb prank. But that's not why I called you back. I'm on a twelve-step program, and Lucy Smithers was one of the people on my list, if you know what I mean."

Marie-Claude knitted her brow in a question, but Kevin did know what he meant. The List was part of the Alcoholics Anonymous recovery process for alcoholics and addicts; it referred to the list of people Jones needed to make amends to - people he had harmed under the influence of addiction. Kevin scribbled a note and pushed it across the desk to Marie-Claude as he said to the telephone speaker, "OK, we're listening."

"I'm sitting in my car right now, talking on a prepaid cell phone that I use for emergencies." Kevin raised his eyebrows but said nothing. There was a long pause on the line. Kevin wondered if he should stop the guy and tell him he was talking to a detective. But he didn't want to lose Jones' momentum, and as Mulally had reminded him, there was no real crime here. He stayed quiet.

"Are you still there?" asked Kevin.

"I knew Lucy in college; I took her on a few dates. I got a little carried away in my room at the frat one night, and she sort of went crazy after. I got two daughters in college now…I know things have changed. But, you know, it was different then, we figured a girl wanted to fight back a little. It was all part of the game." There was another long pause. "And Lucy wasn't even a student."

A glance told Kevin that Marie-Claude's eyes had gone dark; she sat rigid as a stone. Kevin wasn't sure what to do with his hands or his face. He sat just as still, staring at the phone, writing down every word Jones said.

"And Hollingsworth, he fixed it. I'm not sure exactly how, but he gave her some money, made her promise to keep it quiet, and I don't know – it worked. But I look back now…it was bad. Now I see that I was a drunk even then; I just took no personal responsibility for anything." His voice cracked. They heard him take a slow, wobbly deep breath.

"I know the statute of limitations has run out, so I don't face prosecution. But I wanted to call her to make amends. To apologize for being an asshole. I mean, for assaulting her. Honestly, I've been putting it off, looking her up, and I guess it's too late now." Kevin stared at the phone. A glance at Marie-Claude told him she was doing the same; only the firm set of her jawline revealed any emotion.

"But, you know, Hollingsworth – he's a real sadistic prick. I wonder if he knew she was dead when he ordered that bench. You know, he made us send Christmas cards to her family every year, like a subtle reminder that we hadn't forgotten, and that we were holding her to that sick deal. Jesus. And gradually I could see that those cards were also to remind *me* that I owe him.

"It's gotten personal. He wants to buy my family's trucking business. He's one of these private equity douchebags, you probably know that since he's one of your big benefactors – I've seen the red-carpet treatment he gets on campus, and the fact that his mediocre kids keep getting admitted, year after year. Anyway, I don't want to sell, but he's turning the screws on me. And there's no question I've made mistakes running the business." Jones was speaking in a monotone, and the pace of his telling had speeded up. It was almost as if, now that he had started, he wanted to unleash the whole ugly thing. Kevin kept writing, but he glanced up long enough to notice that the tip of Marie-Claude's ear, framed by her smooth chignon, was burning red.

Jones went on. "That's why I know about the statute of limitations. I looked it up when he showed me that bench and I saw the evil look on his face. He's trying to blackmail me, sucker me on the business, and I can't do a damn thing about it."

Kevin wasn't sure what to say; Marie-Claude looked angry beyond words; he didn't think she was capable of speech at all. Trying to end the call, Kevin stammered an awkward, "Thank you for your time." He was about to say, "You've been very helpful," but it just seemed the wrong tone entirely.

"OK, well. I wager you got more than you bargained for from this call. And I guess this conversation is the closest I'll be able to get to making amends to Lucy Smithers. It's the best I can do and I wish to god I'd done it sooner. I'm truly sorry about that night. I've done a lot of things I regret."

Neither Kevin nor Marie-Claude said anything; they avoided each other's eyes.

Jones continued, "Listen, I know you'll do what you have to do, but if you talk to Hollingsworth, I'd appreciate it if you can keep my name out of it. It's probably more than I deserve. But…there's a lot of money on the line." His voice broke, "Jesus, it's my father's business. My brother, our kids." Neither Kevin nor Marie-Claude responded.

"OK. Well, good-bye," said Reuben Jones.

"God speed," said Kevin. He thought of his own father, dying of cirrhosis in a gray hospital bed. Had he gone to his grave with the same deep well of regret?

Marie-Claude reached out one finger, perfectly manicured, and pressed the *Release* button on the speakerphone they had been sharing.

"I need some air," she said, and left the room with her eyes cast down. Kevin stayed for a moment longer, trying to process a deep unexpected surge of shame. He glanced around her crisp office, with its sunny stack of brochures, framed prints on the wall of Marie-Claude smiling with famous, accomplished alumni, and plumped in the other side chair, a needlepoint throw pillow displaying the university crest. He wondered if she had crafted it herself, and thought again about the tribe, the implications about who counted, and who was worthy of belonging. He roused himself and walked quietly out of the office. He didn't see her or anyone else as he left.

As he walked back across campus in a daze, he glanced at his cell and saw a message from Fensbridge. Crap, he had forgotten to follow up on the last one. This message invited him in clipped and formal language to make an appearance at office hours, which happened to be right now. Without really thinking it through, Kevin changed course and headed for the political science building.

Fensbridge's office was so different from the one he had just left. Marie-Claude's space was bright and modern, with just enough room for her desk and two straight guest chairs. Of course, Kevin himself had a metal desk in a bullpen, an open room shared with six other people. Fensbridge, in comparison, occupied a burnished office lined on three sides with bookshelves from floor to ceiling. The fourth wall was mostly windows, half covered in lacy ivy that fluttered in the breeze outside and gave the room a peaceful, sylvan luxury. The room was large enough to accommodate an antique desk, as well as a rumpled sofa and side chairs arranged comfortably on a faded Persian rug. Fensbridge looked up frowning from his computer screen when Kevin knocked.

"Come in, come in," he said, tossing his eyeglasses on the cluttered desk and digging the palms of his hands deep into his eye sockets, covering both eyes completely. He didn't seem to register Kevin's purpose until he put his glasses back on.

"Hello, I'm Detective Kevin Conley from Campus Police. You asked me to stop by."

"Oh, yes, right. You're here about the threatening emails. Have we met before?"

Kevin decided to let it go. He extended his right hand across the desk and said, "I've been on the force for five years; our paths may have crossed."

Fensbridge let a twinkle play across his left eye as he half-stood to shake hands across the massive desk.

"Right, the force. Yes. So, Officer…"

"Detective Conley."

"Of course, Conley. Now what are we going to do about these emails? The woman is clearly unhinged, the frequency is increasing, and I really don't think I need to be threatened in my place of employment."

Kevin decided to play it by the book, stick to the facts and behave as if this were a press conference. He reviewed the situation in a bland voice. "Yes, she has been in touch with several people around the university. We monitor her communications and don't see a real threat there. But as I said, we continue to monitor."

Fensbridge interrupted to wave a loose-limbed hand in Kevin's general direction. "Sit, sit, please."

Kevin sat in the straight chair facing the desk, noting that it placed him lower than Fensbridge's gaze. He continued, "When things reached a high pitch two years ago, we sent her what is called an 'annoyance' communication, drafted by the General Counsel's Office. It's like a 'cease and desist' letter, but less, uh, harsh. It seemed to have some effect."

As Kevin spoke, Fensbridge's brows remained

tightly furrowed, and the edges of his mouth began to turn downward. "She is accusing me of sexual misconduct, which I think is rather harsh indeed. I assure you I take that seriously, and I would think the university would do the same."

"Is there any truth to her accusation?" It was too bald a question, and as soon as he uttered it, Kevin wished it unsaid. A second too late, he recognized the spillover from the other case. It was a rookie mistake from Policing 101. So much for the bland press conference conduct. Dammit.

"I beg your pardon?"

"With all due respect, sir, we deal with sexual harassment, misconduct, and assault cases every week. We can't just assume that every victim is delusional or hysterical. So I have to ask." Kevin knew he was backpedaling; he hoped it didn't show.

"With all due respect my ass. I did not have sex with that woman." Now it was Fensbridge's moment to wish he'd chosen his words better. The echo of the famous line hung in the air. Shaking his head, he said, "I think I met her once. She attended a talk and reception afterward, then contacted me for career advice, which I generously offered in the form of a single email, as I always do when students contact me. And she wasn't even a real student."

Kevin cringed at the term 'real student.' It was the second time that day that an alleged crime victim was presumed to be less important based on her lack of admission to the university. The tribal thing again. It was starting to get extremely irritating. He found he really didn't have the patience to deal with it anymore that day. Better to retreat before things got ugly.

He rose from the uncomfortable chair. "Professor Fensbridge, I keep a file of these communications. If the frequency and tone ramp up again, I will work with the general counsel to send another, perhaps more strongly worded, letter. In the meantime, if you would like to make a statement for the file describing the nature of your relationship with Ms. Sturgis…."

"*We don't have a relationship!*" Fensbridge hissed.

"Sir, if you would like to document this lack of a relationship for the file, and describe the nature of the assistance you provided, perhaps attaching the emails you exchanged on career advice…"

"*Email singular. I sent that harridan one email!*" Fensbridge, jabbing an angry finger toward Kevin, was not backing down.

Kevin was moving toward the door. His prime objective was to leave the room before he lost his temper with this superior prick. He knew better than to take on a tenured professor.

"Attach the singular email you sent, that would be fine. And I will document the information you have shared with me in this meeting. Please do continue to forward all emails you receive from her to me. I think we have the situation under control."

Near the door, Kevin figured he was home free. But Fensbridge wasn't finished yet.

"I disagree. You most obviously do not have the situation under control. I am being harassed and I don't appreciate it. But I can see you are not authorized to actually solve this problem, so I will bid you good day." With that, he swiveled his chair back to face his computer screen, turning his back to Kevin, and began banging his mouse on the desk ostentatiously, his chin jutting toward the screen. Kevin walked out and down the wide, worn marble stairs, breathing slowly and deeply. As soon as he was outside, he sat down and lit up a cigarette. It didn't really help, but it was something.

Kevin waited a day to bring Mulally up to speed on the monuments case. He needed to wait until his own blood pressure returned to normal so he could stick to the facts.

While hearing Kevin's summary of the three phone calls - Finkelstein, Shipley, and Reuben Jones - Mulally reached for his empty coffee mug three times, each time confirming its emptiness. Peering into the porcelain depths the third time, he observed out loud, "Still empty." He raised it to his mouth anyway, stalling.

"OK," he said, "let's break it down. Jones is right about the statute of limitations on sexual assault. Plus the victim is deceased. So there's no path toward prosecuting a crime. The alleged blackmail is not in our jurisdiction. The bench is, all backstory aside, really just an expensive and mean-spirited prank. Buildings & Grounds has already moved it and resodded. I think it's time to let it go."

"I know. I wish it hadn't gotten so dark. This is not what I think of when I think of pranks."

"Yeah," Mulally agreed, "it stinks. I like to think we're better at handling rape and sexual assault now than they were back then."

Kevin thought of his meeting with Fensbridge. "Yeah, I'd like to think so too, but how can we be sure?"

Mulally raised his mug again. "We can't. But we get a lot of training, and we keep working on it. We listen. Kev, take a walk. Get a breath of fresh air; pick up some of that licorice you like. Take your time." It was good advice. Knowing that he had done exactly the same thing the day before, Kevin walked out and did it again.

Sitting on a bench in the quad with an expensive frothy coffee from Starbucks warming his hands, Kevin watched the students rolling through. The young women, purposefully striding between classes in ponytails and jeans, as oblivious to their own beauty as ripe peaches, hatching plans for their bright futures. The young men, shouldering their aspirations as awkwardly as their crooked backpacks. What was going on in all their minds? They had done so many things right already to be accepted to a college as selective as this one. But maybe they had made some compromises too. And all of them had mistakes looming ahead. Power corrupts; power fueled by ambition. A place like this was lousy with it. On the day they were admitted, they had all claimed the tribe, not yet understanding what it might mean. A university man. An alum. An insider - maybe "the man" incarnate. What did "homecoming" mean, after all? They would come home to reunions and networks; already they wore the sweatshirts and linked the golden crest to their profiles and resumes. Some of them would parlay it, using their superhuman drive, into wealth and social standing. They would become important people. And maybe they would use all the influence for good, or maybe they would become blindered, as Mulally had said, mean-spirited. Kevin was thinking that he probably knew more about the shitty sides of all this than most people.

He needed to recalibrate, so he tried to think of all the people on campus he admired; all the people who really had made the world a better place. Creative people: artists, scientists, writers and dancers. He glanced up at the graceful steeple and thought of the chaplain, who had presided over morning service every day for nearly thirty years and was universally beloved for his kindness and his uncanny ability to remember people's names. He thought of the university president who sometimes strolled the quad in the early morning, wearing a Buildings & Grounds jacket and moving unrecognized along the paths, greeting the early workers who prepared the campus for the day.

He dialed Marie-Claude's number; he needed to deliver the news about closing out the investigation. She wasn't surprised, and quite formally thanked him for his help.

"I wanted to tell you, too, that I have been in touch with Hollingsworth," she said.

"How did that go?"

"Well, I managed to suggest that I knew the

provenance of a certain nuisance bench. He laughed; he told me he hoped I understood that it was all in good fun. I didn't let him off the hook that easily; I told him of the labor of removing it as well as the pain it had caused Mr. Finkelstein." She paused.

"Upshot: he has made a very substantial additional cash gift to the university this year." There was a tremor in her voice as she added, "And I have transferred his file to one of my colleagues. I won't be interacting with Mr. Hollingsworth any longer."

She didn't say the size of the cash gift, but Kevin knew that when Marie-Claude said '*very substantial*,' she was talking about more money than he might see in his lifetime. Her tone was polite and professional; he understood this was the end of the line for any thoughts he might have had about lunches, friendship, or something more. She would always associate him with this tawdry case and its rough justice. She wouldn't forget that he knew she had used a woman's suffering as ammunition to blackmail a blackmailer. They had taken a hard look into the abyss together and both had decided to abide. Kevin thought it was probably harder for her because her job actively required her to kowtow to the Hollingsworths of the world. He imagined that she might also have spent part of this mild and sunny day, as he had, reviewing a mental list of the good people in her dossier, trying to rebalance her mental register.

He didn't know what to say, so he tried, "Marie-Claude, you are very good at your job. It's been a privilege working with you."

"Oh Kevin, you are kind," she replied. "I think I have lost my fascination with investigations, though." She laughed – it was a small, dry sound. They both said good-bye, thank-you, and hung up.

Chapter 8 – Second Date

Through the long, lonely weekend that followed, Kevin ruminated on the ugly granite bench, and even more obsessively on the way it had dashed his hopes of connecting with Marie-Claude. His mind replayed images from that last meeting. Her smooth pulled-back hair, the pink tips of her ears as they listened to Rueben Jones, and then the defeated sound of her voice when they last spoke on the phone. It had probably been a pipe dream, thinking that she might be interested in him. Late Sunday afternoon he sat in the Killarney Pub nursing his third beer in front of a Raiders game on the television and contemplating his romantic options. It wasn't going to be Marie-Claude. He didn't have the stomach to go back online again. He thought of Sheila – her open smile and easy manner - and tried to see her sex toys class in a different light. The case of the fake bench had been a grim reminder that, when it came to sex, men could be real assholes. Why should he hold a little female empowerment against her?

He picked up his phone and looked at the blank screen. No notifications; no new messages from anyone. After taking a final pull on his beer, he pulled up her number and texted,

"Hey, been busy but had a great time with you. R u free on Friday? The art institute is open late..."

Within a minute, she replied. "Lemme give you a

call back."

Kevin waited, not sure if that was encouraging. His phone buzzed; her voice on the other end was happy and relaxed. Kevin glanced at the mirror behind the bar, and noticed he was smiling.

"Friday, yeah! I'd love to get together. But…I'm scheduled to host the maker space mixer, first Friday of every month. It's an open house to get more people to join. Do you want to come to that? The thing is, though, since I'm the host, you might be on your own quite a bit. The whole thing dies down by 9:00, so maybe we could catch a drink after?"

So there it was, he had a plan for Friday night. It wasn't the plan he had imagined, which had been more like dinner and a movie. But this was good! A date for Friday night was a win. It made him feel like a man of action, and his father had always said that doing something, even something foolish, was better than waiting.

He figured he would show up around 8:30, toward the end of the event, check out the place, try to steer clear of the dildo section, and then they could go someplace for a bite. Nothing much was happening in the football game, so he killed a few minutes googling pubs in the maker space neighborhood. The googling reminded him of how things had ended with Heather, his girlfriend at the police academy. She was a year behind him in the program, and he'd really liked her, but things hadn't ended well, and with each passing year he understood a little better where he had gone wrong.

Back then, when they were learning various investigative procedures, he used to try them out on himself – simple things like checking a person's credit score, whether they had points on their license, their social media history and prior addresses. Kevin was fascinated by the stuff that turned up – the "digital dust" that people leave behind. He had run a few simple checks on Heather too, thinking that she would want to know what was out there. But it hadn't gone as planned. She wasn't amused; she got pissed and told him she didn't like being surveilled. Told him it was creepy. He apologized and backed off. But a month later when her last name came up in a search during his field study, he couldn't resist following the clue. He found out that her cousin was a low-level sex offender. So then he was in a quandary: did she know about cousin Louie? Should he mention it? He decided to go with the straight and narrow and tell her the truth, but it backfired.

This time she really hit the roof. He had never seen her face so red, her eyes so popping mad. She told him that was it, called him a weasel and a sneak and they were done. She said she'd had doubts about him anyway – he wasn't going anywhere and she was tired of dragging him around like a bag of rocks. She poked her angry finger right into his chest and said, "Don't call me. Don't text me. Don't send me anything. I don't need your fucking apologies. We are done here." She meant it – that was the last time they spoke. It took him a couple of months to get over it, and he'd had other girlfriends since then, but not recently. He still didn't trust his own instincts about what was helpful – which he believed was always his intent - and when his impulse to investigate might cross a line for someone else.

What made him think of that whole saga? He should be feeling good about his plan for Friday night. The guy next to him at the bar was on his phone, obviously talking to his girlfriend or wife. Kevin could tell by the mildly wheedling tone as he repeated, "I'm on my way. I'm on my way." The guy clicked off, put his phone face down on the bar and ordered another beer. He turned to Kevin and said, "Women. Am I right?"

It was a tedious, slow week at work. The kind of week that makes you wonder if your job is a real thing – the six officers, the humming office equipment, the desks and chairs and coffee machine all seemed like tremendous overkill for the absence of any real work to be done. So little happened, he started to worry that Mulally might just amble out of his office and sadly hand them all pink slips. Thanks for your service. Crime has been eliminated; community safety is solved for good. If it hadn't been for drawing class on Tuesday, the gym on the other days, and the light banter of daily office work, he might have committed a misdemeanor himself, just to create a spark.

Adding to the overall malaise, the beeper that Kevin carried, connected to the motion sensors in Waverly Hall, maintained a profound silence. It was all starting to make Kevin doubt his own existence. Inside his left pants pocket, he rubbed his thumb over the beeper several times a day, as if it were a talisman that would bring good luck – like the act of touching it would make it chirp. He even changed the batteries. On Thursday afternoon when he came back to HQ after eating a sandwich at Brad's Place, Rafiq called out to him.

"Conley! Something's been buzzing at your desk. It stopped a half hour ago."

"Shit!" Kevin fumbled inside his pocket, and sure enough the beeper wasn't there. He opened the top drawer of his desk and there it was, silent again. Another situation that proved his general world view that having nothing to do puts a person on the road that leads from lazy to stupid. His mother had been a big believer in the devil's playground, and even though it rankled he had to admit there was wisdom in keeping busy.

Pocketing the beeper, he said over his shoulder, "I'm heading over to West Campus. Be back in an hour." He was too embarrassed to ask for back-up, knowing that whatever activity had triggered the alarm was probably over. Still, he had to check it out. As always, the quad's blue sky and stately buildings exuded peace and timelessness, making Kevin's hurried pace seem out of synch. Over on West Campus, he tried to look nonchalant as he circled the perimeter of Waverly Hall. As he rounded the final corner, he narrowly avoided colliding with Dory, the super, who stopped dead in his path and asked, "How you doing? Have you found the painting?"

Kevin slowed but didn't come to a full stop; instead he brushed past a shrub to pass by her. In a little gesture of police playacting, he checked his watch and raised his eyebrows in concern. Over his shoulder, as he passed, he said, "No, just happen to be in the neighborhood. I'll let you know if anything turns up."

He wished he hadn't run into her; he wanted her to think it was a cold case – a typical minor theft to be documented before everyone moved on. They had gone to some trouble to keep her out of the loop when they placed the motion sensor in the suite. "See you round," he said, as he thought through a new route back to HQ that would keep him out of her nosy sight lines.

As he had suspected, the scene around Waverly was quiet. Whatever had happened was over. He assuaged his frustration by assuming that whatever it was the perps were doing, they would do it again.

Friday rolled around, as Fridays always do. That evening, Kevin had no trouble finding the maker space. It was a sketchy neighborhood, one of those dark borderlands just beyond the low rent housing and adjacent to light industrial warehouses. As he pulled in, he noted that his car was the newest model in the gravel parking lot. He felt antsy. He'd gotten there earlier than planned, so he decided to have a quick beer in the dive next door. It was the kind of place with PBR on tap, mournful Irish music playing low and ESPN on mute broadcasting from a crooked wall-mount. A few regulars looked up at him with little curiosity and no welcome, then went back to looking into their beers. There was a broken jukebox in the corner, dimly glowing under a dusty overhead light. Kevin took a stool at the far end of the bar, away from the other drinkers, and reached for the inside pocket of his jacket, pulling out his investigators pad. The barkeep slid a draft beer to him. Kevin said thanks and laid a fiver on the bar. Flipping open the pad, he started sketching the jukebox, its curves and colors faded with age, its intricate mechanism protected under a glass windshield. It was a beautiful thing; he wondered when the last couple had danced to it. Probably twenty-five years at least.

Lost in reverie, he found himself sketching Sheila's face from memory. He roughed in the curly hair, the glasses, the nice smile. Reaching for his phone, he pulled up her Hinge profile and compared the likeness. Not perfect, but serviceable. No more putting it off. He tapped the fiver on the bar, gave a laconic wave to the barkeep, and crossed the street.

When he walked through the big, reclaimed wooden door, she was the first person he saw. She was wearing black jeans, black converse all-stars, and an oversized gray maker space logo t-shirt. She had torn off the neck band and the sleeves and tied a big knot at the bottom to keep the hem snug around her hips. She had a rose tattooed on her bicep with a trailing vine that led up under the shirt. Kevin felt stodgy and conventional in his jeans, fleece, and sneakers. He was glad to have drunk that beer.

She stepped away from an older guy who looked like an engineer and greeted him warmly.

"Kevin! Hi, I'm so glad you're here. Come and get a beer and let me show you around a little." She gave him a warm, friendly hug. "Are you a big machines kind of guy, or do you like the smaller stuff - looms & Dremel tools and such."

Thinking of the tiny soldering iron she wielded in that website photo, he said, "Big machines, all the way." She led him off, leaning in conspiratorially.

"Perfect timing! I didn't think I could explain the lathe to that guy one more time...He just wasn't getting it."

The place was cavernous, a warren chock-a-block with machines, most of which Kevin could not identify. There was insufficient overhead light and the air smelled of industrial lubricants. As they walked along a central aisle, Sheila helped him see the loose structure behind the place, explaining how the old warehouse had been divided into a grid, with small zones that artisans could rent to pursue their messy projects. Some of the work was strictly functional – there was a metals guy who built specialized machines for industrial production – but a lot of it was pure artistic expression. A giant transformer character, made entirely of bicycle parts, rose menacingly eight feet into the air over one double-wide cube. At the next, a collection of glass lobster buoys was suspended from fishing wire, close enough to clang together in the air currents. Kevin looked down, confirming his prediction with the sight of shattered glass on the floor underneath. It was eerily exciting to walk through the place, so different from ordinary life, dark and messy with creativity. One section caught his eye – a large antique letterpress stood in the center, surrounded by workbenches neatly laid out with fine, sharp tools and stacked thin sheets of copper. A few antique etchings were pinned to a corkboard.

"Who makes the etchings?" Kevin asked Sheila.

"Oh, that's Jason. He's a student at the college as a matter of fact...talented kid. He's not here tonight."

"Jason? Tall, lean, Elvis Costello glasses?"

"Yeah, Jason Whiting. Sounds like the same guy. You know him? Oh, I hope that doesn't mean he's gotten in some kind of trouble."

"I do, yeah. No, we're in a drawing class together. Seems like a good kid. Small world." Kevin tucked away the new information, wondering if Jason's expertise might be useful to his investigation, since the missing art was an old etching.

After a while, Sheila left him to wander on his own while she welcomed other visitors. She would catch his eye with a smile or wave when her informal tours crossed his path. Just after nine, the smallish crowd petered out, and they ended up sitting together on worn-out couches and broken chairs having a final beer with a couple of Sheila's friends, feet propped up on milk crates. There were two women, obviously a couple, who riffed on each other's snarky sense of humor. A quiet, shaggy guy with a pocked face and a shy smile, introduced as the deacon. An older man with full sleeve tattoos and lots of chains hanging from his jeans. Sheila told them Kevin worked at the college, and in this crowd, they assumed that meant the machine shop or grounds crew. Neither he nor Sheila mentioned that he was a cop. The deacon was first to speak to him directly.

"So, new guy. Sheila says you paint."

"Yup," Kevin replied, "mostly I draw, pencil and ink. Walking around here tonight, I can see a lot more possibilities."

"I've got a sweet berth open at the end of aisle nine. Whenever you are ready. Good access to electrical and the power winch; you could stretch your own canvasses, bang some wood together, fling together a collage if you don't like something you've already made…"

He liked their vibe and asked a lot of questions about how the place worked while they all sipped on beers, diet cokes and cigarettes. They were happy enough to talk about what was obviously a passion for all of them. Turned out the seated group was a sort of informal board of directors. The deacon owned the building and used the others as a sounding board for membership outreach, disputes, and new ideas. He called them the Gang of Four, and it was clear they all enjoyed working together, even as they joked that the main advantage of the place was the ability to smoke indoors. Kevin was surprised to find it was past ten when they started to close up.

When Sheila invited him back to her place, he felt a flicker of pride at having passed the test with her gang.

The next morning, Kevin woke up first and decided to make coffee. He rolled out of her bed slowly, trying not to wake her. Scratching his chest, he padded into the bathroom, picking up his pants on the way. He closed the door silently, peed, and inspected his face in the mirror. There was a small bruise on his left clavicle, irregular with bite marks. He remembered it, smiling, as he rinsed out his mouth with toothpaste and an index finger.

When they had walked into the apartment around eleven, she dropped her keys and went straight to the fridge, pulling out two beers. She sat flush against him on the couch, their thighs touching, and pulled out her phone.

"What kind of music do you want to hear? After all that mechanical grinding and whining at the Space, I usually want to hear something soothing." They leaned in close over the tiny screen, idly commenting on the song titles that scrolled by. When he pointed to The Gin Blossoms, she turned and kissed him right on the mouth.

"I love the Gin Blossoms," she said. "So retro."

The signals were all there. Kevin kissed her back, longer, and put his arms around her. He reached one hand down and cupped her ass, turning her closer toward him. She leaned in and put a hand on his thigh. They kissed for a few minutes; his skin tingled when she ran all her fingers up into the hair on the back of his head and kissed his neck. He whispered in her ear, "Are we going to do this?" She whispered back, "Yeah, I'm pretty sure we're going to do this." Kevin reached under her shirt and felt the warm, smooth skin of her back, along with the tight pressure building in his jeans. Kevin pulled her t-shirt over her head; she returned the favor. As each item of clothing came off, they explored the new skin that was revealed. Her rose tattoo turned out to be the beginning of a garland that extended over her shoulder and halfway down the left side of her back, drawn with loving precision. To his relief, they were compatible in bed – he liked to try things one by one to see what a woman responded to; he didn't like to ask. She seemed okay with that, offering little moans, sharp shuddery breaths, or a whispered *yeah*, and reaching out to him in the same way. When she nipped him on the chest near the end, he had pulled away slightly, and looked up to see her smiling mischievously above him. "No biting, I guess," she said breathlessly. He shook his head, as he grabbed her hands and pulled them down, so he could take a nipple between his lips. She laughed.

So, making coffee in someone else's kitchen. It's all about finding the stuff in the least nosy way possible. Is she a coffee in the freezer person? Yes, good guess. He hoped she was also a person who bought ground beans – one less thing to find and one less noisy step in the process. Score two for Sheila. Bottled water in the fridge? No, so probably tap water would be okay. The coffee filters were right on the counter, loose in a wicker basket with a bunch of rubber bands, cocktail napkins, two avocados and three desiccated clementines. Kevin felt victorious when the brewing machine began making that reassuring rumbling/popping sound of coffee on the way. He watched the pot and checked his phone, out of habit and to keep himself from investigating her kitchen. Shit. There had been a series of notifications from the Waverly Hall motion sensor – a series of blips that stretched from two am to 3:15. *Damn*, he'd left the beeper in his pants, out of earshot in the other room. Strike two – he'd missed another opportunity. On the other hand, he wasn't on 24-hour call, and he couldn't feel bad about how he had spent the evening.

He heard the shower start in the other room; temptation flicked him to join her naked body sliding under the water jet but he hesitated.

As a distraction, he surveyed Sheila's small kitchen. The surfaces were cluttered with mail, charging cords, magazines - little wicker baskets were scattered everywhere. One was full of change and paperclips, another full of plastic bread bag closures and twist ties. Draped over a ceiling light fixture was a loop garland made of those weird green Velcro strips that the supermarket wraps around heads of lettuce. Artist or packrat? He reminded himself that he wasn't on the clock, she wasn't a case, no investigative skills required. He checked his phone again and read the headlines. He poured a cup of coffee. He sniffed the milk before splashing some in and sat down at the kitchen table to wait, this time noticing only the artwork that covered the walls in the sunny room. It was an eclectic mix of pastels, oils, pencil sketches, made by different hands but several with the same distinctive scrawled "she" in the corner. The painting she had made on their first date was propped on a radiator, leaning against the wall.

Sheila appeared in the doorway wearing jeans and wet hair. She looked pretty in the sunlight – softer and girlish in her bare feet.

"Hi," she said.

"Hi."

"Coffee. Awesome." She reached for a mug and poured herself a cup. He liked the fact that she didn't say anything else until she had drunk several sips. Part of him was wishing he had left last night, to avoid the clumsy intimacy of morning with a near stranger. But another part still wanted to stay.

"So, hey, I had a great time and I should probably get going…" he said, hoping he sounded as half-hearted as he felt. He was in no hurry to leave.

"Well, OK, but how about some breakfast?" She pulled open a cupboard. "Look at all this cereal going to waste. Toast? Hmm, those clementines don't look too promising." She started heaping choices in front of him on the table. "My plan today is to go for a long walk down by the river. I'm scouting for watercolor spots. Any interest in joining me?"

Kevin considered the idea. He really didn't have any specific plans. He didn't want to impose or seem too eager, and he was intrigued by the idea of painting outdoors – he had always been too self-conscious. But he didn't want to overstay his welcome. Still, a walk wasn't a big commitment, and he could always bail if it got too awkward. *Overthinking again*, he chided himself silently.

"Sure," he said. "Sounds fun. And hey, is 'she' you?" He pointed to the closest drawing, a splashy still life drenched in Caribbean colors.

"It is indeed. She for Sheila. That's me. You can call me that if you like."

It was a warm day for fall, with big rolling clouds that sometimes obscured the sky and other times broke suddenly to reveal a perfect cornflower blue. Sheila was pleasant company. She asked a few questions, but not too many. She offered details about her own life, but not too much. When conversation flagged, she would bring it back to the ideal watercolor site.

"So here's what I'm looking for. A focal point in the distance – like a bridge, a boat, or even a light post or a person on a bench. I think about composition; I definitely want some organic shapes – trees or big plants.

"I want places that people will recognize, because it increases the commercial value of the piece, but I always want to capture a familiar scene or a landmark from a new perspective. Often higher or lower; or maybe much, much closer."

"So you sell your work?" he asked.

"Sure," she said, "if I can find anyone who will buy it. I show in a couple of gift shops around town and I have an Etsy store, like everyone else. I generally don't take commissions – that's too risky for me, because I must be true to my own vision."

Kevin surveyed the landscape with new eyes and

pointed out a few possibilities.

"And of course, it has to be someplace that you can set up an easel without killing yourself."

"Don't you feel a little exposed?" he asked.

She cocked her head at him. "The older I get, the more I realize that nobody really cares what anyone else is doing. People are generally pretty self-absorbed, don't you find? And then again, when people do stop it's usually because they are fascinated. And that can be fun."

"Not distracting?"

"Sure, but I don't mind. It proves the point that art is a great connector. Most people walk around their neighborhood all the time, running errands or whatever, and they don't remember a thing. But that one day when they stop to chat with a painter? That's a day they will remember."

"I never thought about it that way. For me, drawing is more of a private thing. Setting up an easel outdoors feels like attracting attention that I'm not sure I really want."

"Hmmm. Maybe that's the detective in you. You prefer observing the world from the shadows."

He looked at her, thinking that was pretty damned perceptive.

"And you prefer to put it all out there," he responded.

Laughing, she nodded. "To me, it's like exercising. At first very uncomfortable, painful, and awkward and later it gets awesome. Tell you what, we'll find three great spots, pick the best one, and then schedule a time for next week when we can do it together. It will be easier with two. You'll see."

He nodded.

"So what did you do with your PaintBar project," she asked.

"Still in my trunk."

"In your car?" She was incredulous.

"I've got a bunch of pieces in my trunk."

"Hmm. More evidence for my theory that you keep your work in the shadows. I'm intrigued. Why the trunk?"

"I'm not sure really. I just started storing stuff in there. I guess it doesn't take up space in my condo, which is pretty small, and also, I don't have to keep looking at it. I would rather wait and look back at it later when I have some distance. I don't focus on the mistakes as much."

"I feel that," she said. "But you never display your work? Hang it on the wall?" He realized it hadn't occurred to him to do that. He thought back to the jumbled warmth of her apartment and compared it to the stark anonymity of his own.

"Maybe I should do that," he said. But he thought instead of getting some "real" art – go to the university museum gift shop and get some prints from artists he admired.

Chapter 9 – Murder

The rest of the weekend passed in a haze of errands, laundry, and football on TV. Kevin's whole outlook had changed though – things had gotten off to a promising start with Sheila. She was easy to get along with, friendly, fun, interesting, sexy. Yes, things were looking up.

On Monday morning, Kevin pulled open the door at CAMPO headquarters with a spring in his step. There was no one at the front desk, which was unusual, and when he turned the corner into the bullpen, three sets of eyes looked up. Rafiq, with a swift jerk of his head, motioned Kevin toward the coffee room and rose to join him there.

"Something's up." Rafiq said, as they went through the motions of pouring coffee. "Hamish is in there with the chief." They all knew who Martin Hamish was. A homicide detective on the city force, he had worked his way up from beat cop over a thirty-year period. His square face and buzzcut were familiar from a handful of grisly press conferences on local TV news; he had a knack for saying very little but implying that the details were more than your average citizen could handle. Among cops, he also had a reputation as a mean, sharp-tongued shark…one of those guys who would cut you down to size in a way that everyone would laugh off – and you damn well better laugh along with them while you polished up your resume. Kevin could remember stories from his father about guys who effed up once – that was all it took. His dad used to say that Hamish could have coined the phrase "everything is evidence," and seemed to apply that worldview with equally harsh, exacting terms to criminal suspects, bystanders, his own investigative team, even his family. He'd been married a few times – Kevin vaguely recalled some kind of wager on how long the third wife would be able to tough it out.

So if Hamish was in Mulally's office, things were about to get interesting and probably not in a good way.

"Chief wants you in there asap. I was gonna wait five more minutes and text you."

Kevin glanced at his watch as he poured a cup of coffee by rote. "It's not even nine – I'm running early."

Rafiq shrugged, "What can I say? Go in and find out what's the big mystery."

Kevin set the coffee on his desk on the way by, realizing it wouldn't please Mulally if he strolled in with a fresh cup.

He knocked before opening the office door and poked his head through the gap. "You wanted to see me?" Mulally and Hamish were both standing, looking across the desk at the computer screen together. Hamish was two inches shorter than Mulally, burnished and solid as if he'd spent his life digging ditches.

"Yeah. Shut the door. Detective Hamish, Detective Conley." Both men nodded as they shook hands, signaling a shared manly disdain for small talk.

Hamish got right to it. "Here's the deal," he said, tapping a small tablet in his left hand. It was a high-tech version of Kevin's paper notepad, right down to the wide blue lines printed on a yellow screen. Kevin could see icons representing loose-leaf holes drawn along the left edge, and scribbled notes. "I'm on the homicide beat."

Kevin nodded slightly, wearing his best poker-face and standing at five degrees off military attention. No genuflecting; no false surprise; all business.

"One Tiffany Matthews, age twenty-seven, found dead behind a club downtown Sunday night. Apparent opioid overdose. Single; lived over in Centerville."

Mulally cut in. "Detective Hamish thinks the situation is suspicious – not your typical OD. She appeared to have been dumped there, hadn't been seen earlier in the club, had multiple contusions like she had been in some kind of fight."

Hamish raised an eyebrow at Mulally as if accusing him of stealing his thunder; Mulally returned his level gaze. Fascinating power dynamics, Kevin thought, and tucked the image away so he could share it over a beer with Rafiq later on. Hamish went on, "So anyway. We found her phone in her jacket. Checked her calendar to see who she might have been with or planning to see. Turns out she had an appointment on campus a couple nights ago.... Friday at two in the morning. That's a bit odd, don't you think?"

Kevin was starting to make the connection. "Was she a student? Did she work here?"

"Neither one; no connection to the university." Mulally had, of course, checked this right away.

"And I'm guessing the appointment was at...Waverly Hall 12C," Kevin ventured.

"Exactly. I understand you have the apartment under surveillance?"

"Right. And it did trigger the motion sensor a couple of nights ago, but we didn't make it there in time."

Hamish pointed to the screen. "Yeah, we were just looking at the sensor log. Looks like there have been two missed signals."

"That's right. It hasn't been a high priority; just a missing artwork and some noise complaints."

Mulally backed him up, "We didn't have a 24-hour watch on it. This changes things."

"Any idea what she may have been doing there?"

Kevin responded, "None. But if she was there,

she would be the fifth person. My theory was that it was just booty calls – poor key management by the super creating an opportunity. As the chief said, this, ah, changes things." Kevin was thinking back to Fensbridge, the student Amanda, and the two strangers he'd seen on his stakeout.

"It could be a weird coincidence. But not many twenty-seven-year-old women have two a.m. appointments on campus in their date books." Hamish made the observation sound ominous, which of course it was since Tiffany Matthews was dead.

Mulally pulled up Kevin's reports; they were mercifully up to date. The reports corroborated the discussion - nothing had happened on the case for the past two weeks. Nothing but the two missed signals, that is.

Kevin asked, "What else do we know about her?"

"No priors. Family up in the north lake area. Went to state college, worked for an animal shelter in the city. But she was hanging out with some unsavory types. Roommate has been picked up on a couple of minor drug charges. Most of her social media posts are about partying."

Hamish pulled up a picture of her on his tablet. It was a classic Facebook shot of a smiling girl looking sweaty and plastered, wearing a yellow lei and holding a red party cup high in the air. Tacky and a cliché, but Kevin couldn't help thinking also, *full of life*. Who knows, if he had gotten that signal, maybe this girl wouldn't be dead. She might be in some other kind of trouble, but other kinds of trouble can be fixed. This was one of the tough things about police work: you could never be vigilant enough. You were constantly in conflict with yourself about how much of yourself and your time you should invest; how much of that weight you could bear.

Kevin adjusted his posture, noticing he had slumped as he thought about the dead girl, Tiffany. The big dreams her parents must have had, naming her that.

So now this was an investigation for real, and a complicated one at that. Top priority on the apartment motion sensor, and the city cops would want to keep abreast of the surveillance. Whatever was going on in 12C might unlock something in the murder investigation. As he pondered, Kevin heard Mulally and Hamish jousting over jurisdiction and the chain of command. Bottom line, they needed to maintain good relations and Kevin knew Mulally wouldn't want any threat of violence getting closer to campus.

In his more reflective moments, Kevin believed that part of his decision to stay at the university was to shield himself from the worst cases of police work. His dad had been a homicide detective for a few years, and even as a kid Kevin could see it had eaten him up inside. In trying to protect his family, his father would beat back what he had seen until he almost didn't speak at all. When he was promoted to captain they transferred him to the auto theft unit, and things had lightened up a bit – but not really. Homicide was the glamour job; the job that other cops envied. And recognizing that he couldn't handle the stress had brought him low. Kevin never believed it was cirrhosis that killed him; instead, he'd been crushed by having seen too much human evil. His father's disillusionment with people and the corollary disappointment in himself, never acknowledged or discussed, was a palpable force in the house. For Kevin's mother, the years of not knowing where her husband was, what danger he was facing, and where the haunted bitterness was coming from exactly, seemed to swallow her up as well. Kevin was convinced that her dementia was a response to that. Being kept in the dark had become her destiny.

Kevin had admired his father. He saw his incredible commitment to service and wanted to be that way too – but he also shied away from the worst of it. Not wanting to be dragged down by his father's demons, Kevin had chosen a path that felt safer, further from the cliff edge. But maybe the demons come and find you. Standing in Mulally's office face to face with Hamish felt like one of those moments.

"What did you say about five people?" Hamish's voice pulled Kevin out of his reverie.

"Five people have been in the apartment." Kevin listed them –Fensbridge and Amanda by name, including a quick description of why he thought they were there; the big woman and the squirrely man by description. Tiffany Matthews. "And the super, Dory Johnson. The Chief ordered a financial transactions log on her at the same time that we installed the motion sensor – we haven't gotten the data yet."

"What implicated the super?" Hamish asked.

"She called in the original complaint about the missing artwork, but since then she's been back and forth between stonewalling and misdirection. She pointed a finger at the cleaning crew," said Mulally.

"Got it," said Hamish, rolling his eyes. "OK, the three names we know are officially 'people of interest' on this case. We need to start monitoring any significant movements – if they leave town, etc. Follow up on that transactions log, and order the same for the other two. Any chance we can get phone records?"

Mulally broke in, "Technically, we haven't directly observed Fensbridge at the scene."

Hamish dropped his chin and looked at Mulally from under the hood of his brows. He went straight to the point. "So you're saying it's harder to investigate a member of the faculty, as compared to say a student or a building super?"

Mulally looked straight at him. "I'm saying his presence in the apartment is conjecture." The steadiness of Mulally's gaze tingled the hairs on the back of Kevin's neck.

Hamish backed off. "Monitor the other two. If

Fensbridge is involved, we'll know soon enough."

So they worked out a plan. CAMPO would create a 24-hour call duty on the motion sensor. Whoever was holding the beeper could not be more than fifteen minutes from West Campus. Any signal would be called in to the city; a combined team would respond. Hamish's team would begin interviewing all the people close to Tiffany Matthews. They would pull the phone records on the super's office line, though they all agreed that with everyone using personal cell phones, it wasn't likely to reveal much. They exchanged data on how they would communicate progress.

Mulally scratched his chin stubble and said, "Inside the campus force, we need to maintain strict confidentiality. No mention of murder; this needs to remain a case of theft."

"Don't trust your guys?" Hamish asked.

"I do trust my guys, but murder is above our pay grade, if you know what I mean. We need to know a lot more about what's really going on before we let people connect the school to the murder of a young woman. Everything we've got now is circumstantial – she didn't die here; it's not our case. It's your investigation; we want to assist, but let's keep it quiet. News travels fast inside these gates."

There was a pause as each man contemplated the complexity of jurisdictions, politics, and optics. Nobody wanted to end up on the front page of the Tribune.

"Fine with me," Hamish finally said. He gestured to the bullpen outside the office. "You manage your guys your way. But let's face it - everybody out there knows I'm a homicide cop. You figure it out."

The basics were settled. Hamish turned to leave and said to Kevin as he reached for the door, "I knew a guy named Conley on the force several years back. You look like him."

"Yeah, that was my father."

"Good man. I didn't know he had a kid in the biz. If you want to come down to HQ and sit in on any of the investigative interviews, let me know."

Kevin said, "Thanks, I will. That sounds good."

Hamish headed straight through the bullpen to the exit door, not pausing to look right or left as he strode through the space.

After they heard the main door close behind him, Mulally said, "You know, it's lucky you didn't respond to those signals. There's no telling what you might have walked into. I don't like this at all."

Kevin stayed silent, his head still reeling at the speed with which this had turned from an intriguing nuisance case to murder. Could Fensbridge really be mixed up in this? Dory? It was a whole different ballgame.

"Jesus," said Mulally. "OK, let's pull in the guys and get the duty roster set up. We'll just tell them the art was more valuable than we realized, so we're raising the priority. I mean it about confidentiality, Kevin. Only you and I can know about this. It's way too hot."

Kevin nodded, "You got it. You know I'm not the chatty type."

Mulally shook his head wryly. "That's true. I mean it though - not even Rafiq can know." He paused. "You get first crack at the prime times on the motion sensor duty sheet, if you want it."

Kevin bristled at the implication. Of course he wanted it. It was his case. What the hell did Mulally mean by that? Kevin wondered if his earlier thoughts about demons had been written on his face somehow.

"Yeah, I want the prime slots. I want to solve this thing."

"Good man," Mulally nodded, and Kevin heard the echo of Hamish's comment about Kevin's father. He wondered if this would turn out to be his big break or his worst nightmare.

Chapter 10 – Jason Knows Etchings

"Jason!" It was Tuesday night, and Kevin had arrived early at drawing class hoping to have time for a few words with the kid. He slid into the next chair over. He was still tickled by his "small world" discovery about Jason and the maker space, holding onto the tantalizing possibility that Jason's knowledge of etchings might serve some purpose. Follow every lead, so to speak. Mindful to focus only on the theft, Kevin thought he was choosing his words carefully.

"Small world – I was over at the maker space last weekend and I saw your spot."

A look of alarm passed over Jason's face. "What do you mean? What makes you think I have a spot there?"

Kevin was puzzled; he hadn't expected a negative response. "I was at the open house taking the tour, just checking things out in general and a friend mentioned you."

"Jesus, are you like stalking me or something?"

"No, man. I was there with a friend and she was showing me around. I noticed the etching press because it looks cool, so I asked about it. I have an interest in etchings for a case I'm working on. Anyway, she told me it belonged to a student named Jason. I put the rest of it together myself. Like I said, just a small world." Kevin wasn't sure why he was backpedaling; was Jason just overreacting because he was a cop? Being around cops could make people nervous; it dredged up guilty feelings. But he hadn't seen that in Jason before.

"It's called an intaglio press," Jason said sullenly. "It's an antique."

"Like I said, it's cool. I see why you like it."

"Who's your friend?" Jason asked.

"Why do you want to know?"

"Well, my privacy wasn't respected so why should your friend's be?" asked Jason, with all the logic of a little brother in a sibling face-off.

"OK, look, sorry man. I didn't mean to start something. Forget I mentioned it."

But having made his point, now Jason was intrigued. "What's the case?" he wanted to know.

"I thought you didn't want to talk about it?" Kevin retorted, aware that now he sounded like a brother in pointless pissing match.

"That was about my privacy. Which is gone. So now I'm curious about your case and your interest in etchings. Which I know quite a lot about." He was still a little sniffy.

At that moment, the instructor officiously clapped her hands, her normal routine, signaling that it was time to stop the chit chat and get started.

"We can talk about it during the break," Kevin said in a whisper.

The model walked in. It was a girl this time – a young woman. The instructor had set up a raised platform, loosely draped in pale muslin. The woman dropped her pink robe in a heap along the edge of the platform, and lay down on it, on her left side with her left arm stretched straight above her head. She rested her head on the upraised arm and placed her other arm comfortably along the curves of her body, with her right hand falling slightly forward across her thigh. She trained her gaze at a point above Jason's head. The instructor walked toward her and asked, "Do you mind if I drape the robe across your hip?"

"Go right ahead," she said, lifting her arm to hold it in place.

Once the robe was settled, the instructor addressed the class. "Please begin." During drawing sessions, she often acted as if there was a shortage of words in the universe.

Kevin stretched his hands in an inside-out cats-cradle gesture, rolled his neck, and flexed the fingers of his left hand. He picked up the charcoal, wondering why Jason was so tetchy. He seemed too young to have a lot of secrets. But right away his attention was drawn by the way the woman's upper breast fell gracefully, almost concave along the top as gravity drew it down. It was so unlike a caricature of a breast; so organic. He was glad that the robe concealed her pelvis – the brief sight of her rounded hip had made him think of Sheila lying asleep in her bed in the early morning light. As he sketched, getting the main curves right before filling in the details, he gradually stopped thinking about any of these things and slipped into the zone, where it was just his hand, his charcoal, and the technical challenge of getting it right. When the instructor called out softly, "OK, let's take a break," and the figure model sat up to stretch, Kevin awoke as if from a dream.

Jason asked, "You going out for a smoke? I'll come along." Kevin nodded, not quite ready to break the spell. But as always, the sounds of scraping chairs, student chatter, and the bracing air outside brought him back quickly to reality.

They stepped away from the main doors and Kevin reached in his shirt pocket for the pack. He stuck his other hand in his pants pocket, touching the silent beeper that rested there. He wondered what would happen if he just dropped the whole subject of etchings – sometimes you could learn more by not pressing.

"So why are you so interested in etchings?" Jason got right to the point. Kevin smiled internally, chalking up a point for his own professional instinct of not pressing, and because the question reinforced Kevin's gut instinct that there was no guile in the kid. He figured there was no harm in sharing some basic information.

"There was a theft of an antique etching from the university's art collection. Kind of a minor work."

"And you want to know who might fence it?" guessed Jason.

"What do you know about fencing?" Kevin was surprised by the speed with which Jason had homed in on the criminal possibilities.

"Touché!" Jason smiled, goofily imitating a swordplay lunge. "Seriously, is that it?"

"Well, usually the motive for theft is money. I figure if someone wanted to sell it, they wouldn't use a local guy. Too close for comfort."

"Dude, nothing is local anymore. It's all online."

Oh shit, of course, thought Kevin. "But you can't just put an image out there with the name of the artist. The true owner could find it too easily."

"Right," said Jason, "but it's a little different with etchings since there are multiples of every work. Etchings are, by definition, copies, since they are prints made from metal plates. There are often a few hundred in circulation. Good prints are numbered. So you have to know the artist and number to demonstrate solid authenticity and provenance. Lesser prints are not numbered – they don't go for as much."

"Gotcha. So the seller would have to be careful about the timing, I would think. If a print was stolen, and then one from the series showed up on the market, it would still be suspicious."

"Yeah, for sure. Because the investigators would be looking – at least for a while – for the piece to appear.

"Investigators? Is that normal for an etching, one of hundreds of copies like you said?"

"Depends on the piece. The investigation would

usually be conducted by the insurance company, to make sure it isn't a scam by the insured. You know, somebody who knows what they're doing will know that some numbered prints have been lost to time, and they might alter the number on the stolen print and act like all '*Eureka! We found this missing link.*'"

It was hard to see how this arcane print and the murder could possibly be connected. Kevin was starting to wonder about a different question. "So how did you get interested in this stuff? Aren't you a little young to be like one of those twins on the Antiques Road Show?"

"Oh, you mean the Keno brothers. Right. That's furniture, man. Not art." Jason was dismissive.

"Sorry man, I should have known you'd be a big art snob," Kevin needled him.

"My dad is a fan of those big flea markets, and he would always drag me along. One time we found a bunch of plates for like five bucks and I was fascinated. He bought them for me, and then we tried to figure out how to make prints. Eventually we found an old intaglio press and I was in business. It's a lot of fun. I have a special stamp that I put on them with the real year, and my dad writes up a little something about the history, source, or provenance of the plates – whatever research we've dug up – so that no one mistakes the prints for forgeries. It's a hobby we do together."

"What's wrong with baseball?" Kevin asked, and then immediately wished he hadn't when he saw Jason wince.

"Yeah, he likes that too but it's not my thing."

Kevin changed tack. "Why so secret about the maker space, if you don't mind my asking?"

Jason hesitated. "Umm. Well, sometimes this place sucks, you know? There's a lot of pressure, not just for grades, but for everything. It's hard to fit in on the one hand, and I'm not really sure I want to, on the other. My roommates are assholes." He shrugged. "The fact that I

like to nerd out on printmaking – I kind of like to keep
some stuff for myself. Plus, it's not exactly a girl magnet, if
you know what I mean."

Kevin nodded. Sometimes he forgot what it felt
like to be eighteen and away from home, even though he
was surrounded by these kids every day.

"So who's your friend? At the maker space?"
Jason wasn't giving up on that one.

Kevin decided he owed him an honest answer.
"Do you know Sheila?

"Oh yeah, she's the bomb. She's super nice.
Reminds me of my mom. Is she like your girlfriend?"

Kevin blushed and said, "We've hung out a few
times."

Jason nodded, a man of the world.

"If you want, I could scan the sites for that
etching. Text it to me and I'll check it out."

Kevin took his phone number and texted over the
image he had gotten from the curator.

"Looks like 18th century. Maybe even a Vien?"
Jason said.

"Bingo!" Kevin said. "That's remarkable, man –
what an eye! That's exactly what the curator said." Kevin
was truly delighted. It wasn't the first time that he'd been
surprised by the peculiar depth of obscure knowledge of
someone at the university, and it always lifted his spirits in
a way that he couldn't quite describe. It was one of the
things that kept him doing this job – he couldn't really
explain it, but he loved stumbling across these eddies of
human knowledge.

Jason was tickled and held out his hand for a
victorious first bump. "The light is too weak out here right
now; I'll look more closely tomorrow."

Just then the lights blinked, a reminder from the
instructor that break was ending. They turned to go back
to class.

"Well, next time you're going to the Space, let me know. I'll come over and show you my etchings." Jason laughed at his own joke. "You know, etchings are cool because when you make the plates, you have to do everything in reverse. Plus you carve away all the material that isn't necessary for the finished print – that becomes the white space. It's a heinous technical challenge. I mostly just deal with the antique plates – clean them up and care for them, do the printing. I've tried doing some etching myself, but, well, so far I think I better stick to drawing."

Kevin nodded. They went back to class, where the instructor had asked the model to turn over. For the remaining forty-five minutes, they drew her from behind. Kevin had some success tracing the curves of her waist and hip, and the concave hollow of her upper ass cheek, and the way the flesh above her spine was drawn down, ever so gently, echoing the natural curve of her breast. The transitions from arm to shoulder to back, and how to capture the weight of her head resting on her arm, that turned out to be the hardest part.

When the instructor announced that class was over, Kevin and Jason said good-bye and headed in opposite directions. Walking back toward headquarters to drop off the beeper before he left campus, Kevin put his hand in his pocket and ran his thumb over the smooth silent plastic fob yet again. He noted the crisp quiet of the evening as he crossed the street and breathed in the deep calm he always experienced after class, like breaking the water's surface after diving into a lake. He felt freshly alive and present in the world, as if all his senses were open.

His mind ran over the disparate clues again; he couldn't imagine a story that would combine a stolen piece of art, oddballs visiting the apartment in the middle of the night, and the shady professor. Why this piece of art? Why was nothing else in the apartment disturbed? On his stakeout, the two people had left the building empty-handed. It didn't add up. He thought of Jason's observation, that to make an etching you do everything in reverse and carve away what you don't need. There were some parallels to police work, but how did you know what to keep and what to carve away?

After leaving the beeper, he continued to his car, where he went around back and popped the trunk. Standing in the glow cast by the interior trunk light, he opened his sketch pad and tore the night's work from it, enjoying the sound of each of the spiral tabs tearing loose. He neatly placed the evening's drawings on top of the stack and closed the lid. The work had felt good tonight. He made a deal with himself that when the semester ended and it was time to submit his drawings from class, he would go through the whole stack and pick something to hang on the wall.

Chapter 11 - Making Deposits

The twenty-four-hour duty roster had been drawn up; the motion sensor beeper had begun making the rounds among the full team. But "ring of art thieves" or no ring of art thieves (murder or no murder), life on campus continued to follow its normal rhythms and routines. Drawing class was on Tuesday evenings; Wednesday mornings were for campstat.

When Mulally came in as chief five years ago, he implemented a version of Compstat. It was a standard of community policing, something Kevin had learned about in his criminal justice program at State, but he never thought he'd see it on the college campus. The idea was to improve public safety by using computer statistics (**comp**uter **stat**istics) to identify spikes in criminal activity and deploy the force accordingly. Kevin was impressed when Mulally first introduced it, but again this morning, he marveled at how something that sounded so rational and grand in concept could seem so mundane in daily practice.

The eight members of CAMPO were packed around the Formica table in their undersized conference room, eyes trained on the big screen in the front of the room. Rafiq was screen-sharing from his laptop, projecting a dashboard of campus report stats (**camp**us **stat**istics).

Standing to the left of the screen, Mulally pointed to datapoints that looked out of whack, including a small spike in purchasing cards expenditures. This was unusual for the middle of the semester. He assigned Kevin to investigate. Kevin kept his face neutral to camouflage his inward groan of boredom. He stroked the silent beeper in his left pocket, willing it to free him from the day-to-day ordinariness of this assignment. His immediate fate decided, he zoned out during the rest of the discussion. As the final order of business, Mulally handed out about fifteen follow-up call assignments, apparently not statistically significant, to respond to the non-urgent requests that had come in since yesterday. Kevin's billet was from the human resources manager in the chemistry department. One Mary Sue Flanagan. Sounded like a cafeteria lady from St. Joseph's middle school. Kevin absent-mindedly started sketching a caricature of a jowly woman in a hairnet while Mulally passed out the rest of the calls and said, "Meeting adjourned."

Scraping his chair against the linoleum, Kevin decided to call Mary Sue first. He deprioritized the purchasing cards using the universal criteria of relative boringness. Mary Sue was available to meet right after lunch; Kevin held out hope that the beeper would intervene before the scheduled time.

Alas, the beeper stayed quiet. Just before one-thirty, Kevin walked across campus to the bulky rectangle of brick that housed the chemistry department. No soaring atria here; as he walked to her office on the second floor, he felt the worn soapstone risers under his feet and admired the antique wrought iron scrollwork that supported the banisters. There was a faint antiseptic tinge in the air.

Kevin knocked on the open office door and stuck his head in. Mary Sue Flanagan bore no resemblance to the caricature sketch he'd imagined earlier. Instead, she was small with straight gray hair cut sharply just above her shoulders, round wireframes, and a pink sweater that looked dusty. On the phone, she had been hesitant to tell him much about her "issue," as she called it. Now she rose to meet him, gestured him toward a straight-backed visitor chair, and silently closed the office door before returning to her desk. As she passed by him in the small space, he detected a faint whiff of tobacco. Kevin introduced himself and waited for her to speak. Instead, she sat silently as a pink rash started to crawl up her pale neck. She cleared her throat.

"Take your time," Kevin said as he pulled out his notepad and pencil. He quickly flipped the page to cover the sketch.

"It's terribly awkward," she said, "and I'm not even sure there's anything…for us to discuss. But, well. I didn't feel right about just keeping it to myself. So here we go." Haltingly, she told the story, with her hands clasped tightly on the desk.

"Last Friday was the last day of work for our tech support guy. He got a new job at a local tech company. Good IT people are so hard to find, so of course my first thought was the difficulty I would face trying to replace him."

Kevin nodded, trying to look sympathetic to the challenge of hiring good tech people, not sure where the story was leading.

"He kept to himself; seemed like a bit of an odd duck. But that isn't really unusual for IT people, is it? They are often rather, um, introverted, aren't they?" She seemed to need encouragement to go on. Kevin nodded again. Mary Sue drew a deep breath and cleared her throat again. The rash on her neck was still moving up, approaching her jawline.

"Over the course of a few years, there had been some comments about his behavior, but nothing that was very specific. Some of the female researchers and students found him, well, disquieting and preferred not to interact with him directly. He spent a lot of time in his office with the door closed, which I always worried would discourage colleagues from asking for his help.

"Anyway. There was a glass pane – a sidelight – next to the door, and people could see in as they passed by in the hallway. About a year ago, as a colleague passed by, she heard him cry out. She glanced in, and he seemed to be in pain. She knocked on his door and popped her head in, you see, just to make sure he was alright. He barked at her, '*Go away, I'm fine. Get out.*' Something like that. I know about this because she reported his rudeness to me – to HR - but that was that. I informed his supervisor and coached him on how to provide direct feedback on our values and commitment to treating all colleagues with respect. I figured that was that."

Kevin nodded again. Where was this going? And how long would it take to get there?

"You know, people are hesitant to talk to HR. I imagine the same is true for your line of work – people worry that talking to HR will make things more serious, I guess. In any case, I heard snippets that he wasn't the most popular person in the department. For example, someone might say they preferred using the coffee pot downstairs at the other end of the department to avoid passing his office. I thought this was just idle chatter. And, as I mentioned, he has left the university at this point."

Mary Sue paused in her story and Kevin noticed the hives had reached all the way around her neck and were covering her ears. Her fingers were clasped so tightly on the desk that Kevin could imagine them snapping like little twigs. He sat still, performing patience, waiting for her to continue. The silence grew.

"After he left on Friday, I went into his vacated office to set it up for a new lab associate who is coming in next week. Space is always at such a premium on campus," she said. Kevin smiled and agreed. She fell silent again.

After a few seconds he asked, "Ms. Flanagan, I

could really use a cigarette. You don't happen to be a smoker?"

"Oh yes, what a good idea. And I can show you his office on the way." She almost knocked over her chair, she got up so quickly. Grabbing her coat and keys in one motion, she was out the door in a flash. Kevin followed.

They walked down the wide gray hall together, its walls lined with posters for upcoming lectures, signup sheets for experiments, the usual obscure academic stuff. Selecting from her ring of keys, she opened a nondescript door about halfway down. Kevin noticed the sidelight she had mentioned, and that the view inside was blocked now by closed mini-blinds. She saw him looking, and said, "Yes, I closed the blinds on Friday." They passed into the room together, and she shut the door behind them and leaned against it, stepping aside to let him move the few steps into the cramped space. Situated so that the occupant faced the door was a heavy metal desk, one of those 1960s models that look like they were made of overstock steel from a Grumman aircraft factory. With just the desk, a tall thin filing cabinet and a bulletin board on the wall, the narrow room felt crowded.

"So. Well, may I suggest that you go around the desk and look underneath. As if you had dropped a pencil or something."

Kevin squeezed around and pulled back the desk chair, squatting down to peer into the knee space. It was dim under there, even with daylight coming through the small window behind him. He reached for his phone and switched on the flashlight. The first thing he saw was chewing gum blotting the hidden surfaces. Then he noticed the carpet under the desk was filthy and discolored. The gunmetal gray sides and interior surfaces of the desk were caked with something that looked slick. There were bits of Kleenex hardened to the metal. Kevin looked up to see Mary Sue Flanagan still standing with her back against the door, looking out the window above his

head. Her face, neck, and wrists were flaming red.
"I think he may have been…*masturbating*." At this point
she almost made eye contact with him. Kevin was still in a
half-crouch, but he steadied himself with his hand on the
seat of the desk chair and sat down into it, looking up at
her. His first thought was, "You think?!" But before he
could say a word, she turned and fled, just a flash of pink
rushing down the hall toward the left.

Jesus, what next? It looked like the guy had been
jerking off into this desk for years. Kevin needed to get
out of the room asap; he really needed that cigarette now.
He turned toward the right as he left the office, thinking
they would both prefer to smoke alone. It dawned on him
that he had just been sitting in that chair. He took a detour
into a men's room and washed his hands.

Kevin found a sheltered loading dock and lit up.
He clenched the cigarette between tight lips, reeling from
both a visceral and moral response. When would the
repulsive afterimage of that desk fade from his corneas?
What kind of sick person jerks off at work, in sight of the
people he works with every day? Was the whole university
lousy with sexual deviants? He dragged on the cigarette
and let the nicotine soothe his agitated nerves. He closed
his eyes for a moment and took another deep pull,
reminding himself that there were over ten thousand
people working at the university, and only a few that
crossed paths with CAMPO. This was a mantra that he
sometimes used to keep himself grounded, and he seemed
to need it more than usual this week.

A bit calmer, he pulled out his pad to take a few
notes and think through his next steps. The guy was gone;
that was the good news. Mary Sue had mentioned
discomfort on the part of his colleagues. Were there any
real complaints? As in *complaint* complaints? HR was
usually good at dealing with personnel questions; her
concern must be whether public masturbation was a
criminal concern and whether there were outstanding

security issues. He would need to look at the HR files, for the perp and anyone else who might have mentioned an issue. He rechristened the perp "Jack," and allowed himself a little snicker at his own joke. Maybe he should check to see if there was unusual turnover among women in the department. Make sure Ms. Flanagan was telling him the whole story when she said people found him "disquieting." Find out how long she herself had been working in the department – and who was there before her. He should check the sex offender registry as well, just in case. Sometimes people slipped through the cracks.

He would summarize his notes for HR; then Mary Sue would need to work with the general counsel and the head of university HR to craft a note to the file, to be used in case of future requests for employment references. They would have to decide whether to inform the dude's new employer – not bloody likely, was Kevin's guess, but that that was outside his bailiwick anyway. Now that the concern had been identified, there was liability. He also needed to go back in the room today to take pictures and file a sitrep – situation report. He was not looking forward to that.

The problem with a case like this was that if anything else should happen in the chemistry department in the near future, this story could be layered on to create the appearance of a hostile work environment – even if nothing had ever been documented. If it could be suggested that Jack's little peccadillo was common knowledge, the risk profile would shoot up, so to speak. And god knows the university did not like risk.

The standards were tightening up fast, which was a good thing, but it made life tricky. Kevin's mind jumped to a story he'd heard in the break room after a recent Title IX training. There was this big freshman writing class – a required course that no one wanted to teach. And there was this one instructor who was always game to do it. He was an adjunct, never moving up the ladder, but he stuck around for years teaching multiple sections of this course. He had just been celebrated for twenty-five years of service to the university when a couple of new, female instructors came forward. It turned out that, while commiserating about their workload over half-caf soy lattes, they had discovered that they each had a student who had transferred into their sections mid-semester, and both students confided tear-stained stories of a "relationship" with, you guessed it. The Title IX office discovered the guy had been deflowering first-year students at a rate of four to five each year – all consensual under the law, but a clear violation of the ethics code. Twenty-five years ago – hell, maybe even five years ago - the punishment would have been a furrowed brow from the department head, followed quickly by a wink and a snicker. The tweedy older dudes in charge would have considered it, while unseemly, also rather impressive, and worst case, a useful life lesson for naive young girls. Not anymore. Kevin remembered seeing the guy walking around with students, usually young women, and envying his warm, easy manner. Now he lived under a gag order and was prohibited from passing through the campus gates. And Kevin himself felt dirty for having envied him.

Kevin crushed the butt under his steel toe, flipped his note pad closed and headed back to Mary Sue Flanagan's office with a heavy step. This one could probably be resolved quickly, but the paperwork needed to be careful and complete. The purchasing card assignment was starting to look good.

Late the next morning, a bell tinkled as Kevin pushed open the Starbucks door. It sounded more enthusiastic than he felt, since he had come to meet Larry Melnick from internal audit to talk about purchasing cards. During the short walk across campus, he had willed the beeper to go off, but it remained stubbornly silent. Kevin didn't know Melnick, but he figured he could pick an auditor out of the usual campus crowd. And sure enough, that had to be him at the table nearest to the cash register. Fortyish, wearing a crisp pink oxford shirt and dress pants tucked into rubber hunting boots in defense against the wet weather.

Kevin approached, "Larry?"

"Yes. Officer Conley? Have a seat. I'm glad you're in plainclothes." The guy kept his voice low as he half-stood, reaching out his hand to shake, simultaneously gesturing to the chair across the table. "Thanks for meeting me here."

"Sure. I understand you want to talk about purchasing cards." Kevin didn't try to conceal the dismissive tone of his voice.

"Right. P-cards." Larry hesitated. "How long have you been with the force?"

Kevin bristled. "I'm a Detective, Lieutenant Rank for the University Police. I've been here for six years. You?"

"Just a couple of years. Before that I was with Deloitte. I worked on the university audit when I was there. To get down to it, the auditors reviewed P-card stats every year and I've kept at it in my job here. I know, it sounds boring even to me. P-cards are in wide distribution – every faculty assistant and junior research coordinator carries one around to make routine purchases. There are hundreds of them in circulation. It's like the 21st century version of petty cash, with even more potential for fraud and abuse, since people are carrying them around all day and, like cash, they can burn a hole in your pocket. It's a small-time crime of opportunity. Part of the reason I wanted to meet here is that this location is on the Top Ten Vendors list.

"The university is paying for everybody's four-dollar morning coffee?" Kevin's basic sense of propriety was mildly offended.

"It's not technically prohibited." Larry made no effort to hide his disapproval, and Kevin grunted in agreement. "The policy is that it's acceptable to cater a meeting that occurs during a customary mealtime – like an early breakfast meeting or a lunch meeting. One potential for abuse is in the definition: what constitutes a meeting? So of course, we look for patterns of the same P-card being used every day for a charge of less than $5. That's just somebody buying their morning jolt on the university's nickel, and that's something that a good manager can discourage pretty easily. We give the manager the data, and we watch the pattern disappear like magic. But that's not the problem. I mean, I wouldn't waste CAMPO time on that." Kevin appreciated that Larry was trying to flatter him.

Larry snapped open his laptop, and looking furtively around, turned it so he and Kevin could look at the screen together across the marble café table. Kevin noticed Larry had chosen a table in sight of the cash register, but with no one seated behind them. On the screen there was a detailed spreadsheet, stamped confidential. "We've completed our audit, and we have a tiered list of interventions where we need the support of University Police. Check out the section on gift cards. Gift cards, by the way, are explicitly prohibited." Larry highlighted a section in the middle of the second page. Kevin scanned the table, which was titled P-card Infractions Summary. It showed Class of Infraction, Number of Infractions, Total Dollar Impact, and Planned Intervention. The numbers were staggering. P-cards were being used to purchase gift cards – 150 infractions in October alone, and 72 of them were in a single department. Ten instances of gift cards being purchased out of state, mostly in consumer electronics stores. One instance where a single person used multiple P-cards to buy gift cards just below the audit threshold, consistently every month for five years, for a total value of $19,000.

Kevin looked up. "You've got my attention."

"Gift cards are the bane of internal auditors everywhere these days. Not exactly glamorous. Perfect vehicle for small-scale money laundering." Larry sighed. "I've been here since nine-thirty watching the cash register transactions. Vendors are not supposed to allow people to use P-cards to buy gift cards. But obviously baristas are a weak link in our enforcement system." Kevin looked at the young woman behind the counter. Piercings, tattoos, ratty jeans. Her hair was dyed yellow and pink in streaks. Heavy eyeliner did not conceal the boredom on her face.

"I haven't seen any suspicious activity yet today," Larry said, looking disappointed. Kevin thought, *everybody loves a stakeout.*

"What comes next?" Kevin asked.

"For every infraction, as you can see, there is a planned intervention. Depending on the seriousness and scale, the interventions range from a stern, documented conversation with a supervisor, to a warning in the personnel file, delivered by the department head and financial manager, all the way up to termination. For the bigger offenders, there is a whole process and different people need to be involved. HR, supervisors, general counsel, etc. Sometimes when we confront the person, things can get a little…conflictual. We like to have security back-up."

"So, I'm the muscle?"

Larry snorted in appreciation. "Well, it's not exactly Goodfellas. I like to think of it more as a unified show of authority, and a demonstration that we have done our homework. There's no weaseling out with lame excuses, like there might be when people are dealing only with close colleagues."

Kevin tried not to let his irritation show. Why had Mulally assigned him to this? If they just needed someone to stand there in full uniform with their thumbs hooked in their service belt and their chest puffed out, a rookie uniformed beat cop could handle it. Straight-up intimidation of petty villains? Kevin knew this was not Larry Melnick's problem. He would take it up directly with Mulally. And like always, his mind was on his real case.

"OK, sounds good. While we're here, I'm working on another case and maybe you can help me out…"

Quickly and with few details, Kevin mentioned his transactions request on Dory Johnson, pinning it to the missing artwork. "Bottom line," he said, "what's taking so long? Can you get it unstuck for me?"

Larry nodded. "Sure enough. Sounds fair. I'll track it down today. An art heist sounds more colorful than P-cards."

"Do you guys have access to phone records, too? I'm having the same problem there."

Larry shook his head in frustration. "Ugh. Central IT manages the old Centrex system we're still using. The data reporting is notoriously clunky, and therefore slow as molasses. And to be honest, no one uses their desk phones much anymore. Everyone uses their cells, on the move. But I know a guy over there, and if you want me to make a call, I'll see what I can do."

Kevin said, "Yeah, thanks man. I appreciate it. It may be a dead end, but I've gotta track it down."

Just then, Melnick nudged his toe hard against Kevin's foot. Kevin shot him a glance, and Larry flicked his head toward the cash register. A well-dressed young guy had just handed over a bright gold P-card to the cashier, asking for a fifty-dollar gift card. The P-card was instantly recognizable, the university crest and logo both jarring and familiar. It was something Kevin had seen a thousand times, never giving it much thought. The barista paused and started to hand the card back with an apologetic smile, when Mr. Smooth leaned in and said something they couldn't catch. The barista's eyes narrowed as she cocked her head. Still leaning intimately forward, Smoothy smiled and cocked an eyebrow. Returning his flirtatious smile, she turned to the register. Kevin stood up as if to get some sugar, so that he could watch the transaction. She swiped the P-card, then swiped two gift cards. One, she handed to the guy along with the P-card. The other gift card she slid into the back pocket of her jeans. It was so simple, and so quick.

"I'll talk to him now," said Kevin.

Larry grabbed his arm. "No, wait. It's better not to tip him off."

"I want to know who the guy is; I'll tail him. I'll call you later." And with that, Kevin was out of the coffee shop. He could see the kid in his tight burgundy hipster pants a few yards ahead, flipping another loop of his scarf around his neck against the cold. Kevin watched him cross the main quad and enter Harker Hall, the grand central building that housed the president's office. As Kevin approached the building, he spied a glove on the ground. He picked it up and walked into the building.

There was a receptionist inside the door. Kevin approached her. "I just saw a guy come in here – he dropped his glove. Young guy, red pants. I couldn't catch him…"

"Oh, you must mean Carmelo Jones. He just came through a second ago. Shall I give it to him? How kind of you."

"Great, thanks." Kevin turned and walked back out the door. He used his phone to look up Carmelo Jones in the campus directory. Admissions Coordinator. Class of 2010. Really, Carmelo?

Heading back to HQ, Kevin thought maybe this P-card gig wouldn't be so bad after all.

Chapter 12 - Downtown Police HQ

On Thursday there were two interviews scheduled at downtown police headquarters. Hamish was seeking background information from some of the dead girl's friends, and he had made good on his offer for Kevin to sit in. Kevin showed up in plain clothes, trying to look nonchalant about his first murder interrogation.

The headquarters building was imposing and modern on the outside, a fortress of tinted glass flanked all around by stainless steel bollards – those waist-high posts that keep vehicles from crashing into buildings. On the campus, most of the bollards were disguised as planters. Here they were sleek and utilitarian, suggesting a phalanx of robotic guardsmen. Three flags waved over the wide entrance — the US and state flags and the classic Viet Nam-era POW-MIA flag. The place sent a chill radiating up Kevin's spine as he pushed through the main revolving door and faced the metal detection apparatus inside.

Once he'd cleared security, he texted Lieutenant Smith as instructed. A burly, untucked guy appeared from an elevator a few minutes later, gesturing for Kevin to approach. "Smitty," he said. "Are you Conley?"

They rose to the third floor together. After the grandiosity of the main foyer, the interior was disappointingly ordinary, with fluorescent lighting and dull, scuffed desks haphazardly filling any available space. Smitty walked him over to Hamish's office and disappeared with a wave, saying, "Have fun."

Hamish was talking on his cell when he approached, so Kevin hovered outside the door until Hamish gestured him inside.

"Yeah. Yeah. OK. Got it. Right. Keep me posted." Hamish tapped the screen of his phone and tossed it on the desk, over a stack of paper.

"Sit, sit," Hamish said. Kevin sat in the only chair – a small, straight-backed chair not unlike the one in his art class. He shifted his limbs awkwardly, trying to find a comfortable position.

"OK," continued Hamish. "The rules are simple. We'll enter the room together. You'll sit back against the wall. I will introduce you as 'Officer Conley' with no reference to your jurisdiction. You do not participate in the questioning – you observe. I'll have a tape recorder, but I can't share the recording with you. That's strict procedure. You can take notes. Got it?"

Kevin nodded.

"Good. We'll debrief afterward."

Kevin nodded again, "It's your investigation, Detective Hamish."

Hamish checked his watch. "It's time. Come on." Kevin followed Hamish into a barely furnished room off the main entrance, labelled only Room 2. The room had four of the same straight-backed chairs he'd just sat in, no table, and no one-way mirror like on TV. A young woman in black pants and a pressed button-down shirt sat in one chair, stiffly clutching the scuffed, faux leather purse in her lap. Hamish pulled up the second chair and placed it directly in front of her, their knees about twelve inches apart. She scraped a few inches back on the linoleum, then leaned away, pulling her bag closer. Kevin took the third chair and dragged it to the wall, just to the left of Hamish's shoulder, so that he had a clear view of her face. He sat down, trying to look neutral, and flipped his pad open.

Hamish pulled a recording device from his pocket, held it up toward her, and said he would be taping their conversation. She nodded, and he pressed a button. He held the device in his hand, clearly visible leaning on his left knee. He introduced himself and Kevin, then asked her to state her name for the record.

"Alison Jenkins."

"And how were you acquainted with the deceased, Tiffany Matthews?"

Alison winced at the mention of Tiffany's name. "She was my best friend from high school."

The detective's interrogation style was simple.

"Ms. Jenkins," Hamish said calmly, "I want to assure you that you are not a suspect in this investigation. You're here today because we're seeking information to bring Alison's killer to justice." He paused, and she nodded nervously, her eyes darting toward Kevin.

Hamish continued, "I want you to tell me anything you can about Tiffany. It is early in the investigation, and we don't know what might be useful."

He listened closely to everything she said, then followed with questions that mostly consisted of a single word, as in, "Boyfriends?" "Parties?" "Enemies?" "Arguments?" At times when Alison stopped speaking, Hamish would tilt his head a few degrees, and Alison would start talking again, providing more detail. It was exciting to watch the way she responded to his simple cues. There was an attentive stillness in his posture; an electricity that even from behind, Kevin could feel between them. Seated at his off-kilter angle, Kevin couldn't discern what expression Hamish wore on his face, beyond the head tilt, but it was working.

"Drugs?"

"We tried pot together for the first time when we were fourteen, during a break at weekend math camp. We weren't *that* nerdy – our parents signed us up, thinking we'd make honor roll after or something. The kids from the next town offered weed, we smoked behind the church, it was fun. T liked it."

Hamish's head tilted slightly.

"She acted up a little during class after. Mr. Yuli, the teacher, told her to stop giggling. She was acting happy, talked too loud at pizza after. Maybe it sounds weird, but Tiffany cracking jokes and being happy wasn't usual. For whatever reason she went home and told her mother, who hit the roof. That's when Tiffany decided her mother was a total bitch, and that pot was the secret to making herself happy. She started smoking a lot, more than me anyway." Alison sighed. "She started hanging out with other kids and trying harder drugs, but we stayed friends. Then she went to State, I went to St. Benedictine, and we mostly fell out of touch except for some Facebook messaging."

Hamish broke his streak by asking a full question, "Did you both have friends at other colleges in the area?" He mentioned three other colleges within fifty miles, including the university. Kevin started to sweat – Mulally would have had kittens if he had heard Hamish mention the university so baldly in this setting.

Alison just shook her head and said, "No way. We didn't have the money; we didn't know anyone at those fancy places. We were just regular kids."

"When did you see Tiffany last?"

"Must have been last winter. We'd get together in our old neighborhood around the holidays, so I only saw her around a couple times a year. From what I could tell on Facebook, her new best friend is Christine. I've met her once or twice. She's a big partier."

When her words dried up, Hamish nodded. In a manner that was surprisingly gentle, he thanked her for her time and assured her that they would find the perpetrator. He told her she had been very helpful, and she shrugged, saying, "I wish I knew more. It's just awful. I can hardly believe she's gone."

She placed her handbag over her shoulder, squeezing it tightly against her side.

"Am I free to go?"

Hamish nodded, then rose to open the door for her. She passed through the door as if another minute would have seen her locked up. Kevin was amazed anew to see that even the innocent, when walking in the halls of criminals, would begin to doubt the condition of their souls. It would probably be a few hours before Alison would feel like herself again.

The two men crossed the hall to debrief back in Hamish's office. After the austerity of the interrogation room, Kevin noticed how the space was cluttered with overburdened bulletin boards and stacks of files. Kevin took in the thumb-tacked notices, photos, dated policy memos, and Most Wanted posters, including some jokey replicas from old Western gunslinger television shows. His eyes paused at one of the corkboards, which displayed a collection of arm patches from other forces around the country, a common hobby among cops. Hamish noticed his gaze and opened a desk drawer to flip Kevin a patch from his unit. Kevin caught it and smiled. "Thanks, man."

"OK. What did we learn?" Hamish asked.

"The drugs are a thread. Tiffany was okay with taking risks. She wasn't secretive by nature."

Hamish nodded, "Yup. Good summary. Anything else?"

Kevin added, "I believed her when she said they were not in touch. It felt authentic."

Hamish nodded. "Yeah. Smitty is digging into her social media accounts for more connections; we can confirm that stuff pretty easily."

A deputy brought in two cups of thin coffee and told them Christine had arrived and was waiting in Room 5. Hamish nodded and reached for a cup, taking a deep pull.

Hamish said that Alison's story corroborated what Tiffany's mother had provided; he was clearly disappointed that Alison had left no new hooks or jagged edges to investigate. Taking a final gulp, he rose, tossed the cup in the bin, and led Kevin to room five, which looked exactly like room two. Kevin knew the drill now - he moved his chair to the back and observed Christine, who looked a little older than Alison despite her jeans and hoodie. Her eyes were rimmed dark, her hands thrust deep into her pockets and her legs were extended as she slouched in the chair, black boots crossed at the ankle. Hamish's approach was the same and Kevin's pad began to fill with notes.

"Oh God, I loved Tiff," Christine said. "We worked together at the shelter. She was so great with dogs, a dog whisperer! They can always sense a good heart. And she was funny too! It didn't always come through in her standup, but I thought she was ballsy for doing it."

"Where did she do stand-up?"

"You know, the open mics. Improv, Laffers, The Kitchen. We would watch, hang out with the other comics. But she had bad stage fright and needed something strong before going up there."

"Did she use a lot of drugs?"

"She liked to party. Nothing specific; tried whatever was on hand. She wasn't an addict if that's what you mean."

"Boyfriends?"

The right side of Christine's mouth lifted, like half a smile. "Honestly, she wasn't like that. She liked to party and hang out with the gang, but there was no particular guy. Not that into sex."

Hamish must have raised an eyebrow or something because Christine suddenly sat up straight. She leaned toward Hamish, hands still in her pockets. She looked him dead in the eye as she said, "I really noticed that about Tiff because I am. You know, into it."

Kevin watched as they held that silent, still gaze

for a long beat; there was nothing subtle in either the challenge or the invitation.

And then Hamish said, "Enemies?"

"Why would a great girl like Tiff have enemies?" she said, sitting back abruptly with a peeved expression. Her chair scraped back on the floor. Kevin felt her disappointment in failing to get a rise out of the detective.

"Money trouble?"

Christine snorted. "Sure, of course she had money trouble. She was working at an animal shelter and doing standup for free beers. She had talked about a couple of harebrained schemes for making some bank, but I talked her down."

"Such as?"

"Stripping for one. The money's great, but a person has to protect herself from that kind of energy. Tiffany was too gentle for that crowd; that's why she liked the dogs."

Hamish thanked her for her time and assured her, as he had before, that they would do everything they could to find the killer. Christine looked skeptical, but she nodded and offered a tight smile as she headed out.

Back in the office, they reviewed what they had learned. The comedy angle was new; Hamish decided to send Smitty to the clubs Christine had mentioned and ask around a bit. Kevin asked if the club where she had been found was a comedy club, but it wasn't. It was The Rock, a small, divey music venue where hard rock and punk-influenced bands played.

"That's surprising. Neither friend mentioned that Tiffany was a music fan," Kevin observed. The Rock was the kind of place that had a very loyal clientele of mostly local kids who liked their music loud and fast. They slammed around in a mosh pit to work off their frustrations.

"Maybe she was dumped there. Probably died somewhere else," Kevin offered.

"That tracks." Hamish leaned his chair back and put one foot against the edge of his desk. "I liked that story about the stakeout, how you identified those two suspicious characters in Waverly Hall."

"Thanks, man."

"You ever feel like you're wasting your time over there on CAMPO? I mean, it must be pretty dull." Hamish had a half-smile on his face.

"You'd be surprised," Kevin responded.

"You're right. I would be. The whole set-up looks like small potatoes to me. Like you're sitting in a kiddy pool when there's an ocean of crime that needs to be solved." Hamish had stopped smiling.

"With such a small force, I'm juggling three or four cases at a time," said Kevin. He was aware of his urge to impress Hamish. "Some are small, others not so much. This week I'm working on a couple of embezzlement investigations. You never know what's next." He glanced at his phone. "In fact, I need to get back over there. Thanks for the opportunity to sit in. I learned a lot from your interrogation method."

Hamish brushed it off. "Pfft. Character witness 101 stuff. But I'm glad you could come down, get a taste of the real deal. We'll check in Friday on progress; next week we talk to the other two known leads."

"Amanda Herring and James Fensbridge," Kevin supplied the names.

"Right. Later, Conley." Hamish turned his attention to the screen.

Kevin saw himself out. As he walked toward the exit, he took in the downcast demeanor of the uniformed officers, the frown lines etched on their faces and the slumped postures of the dispatchers and support staff. What a grim place to show up for work every day, he thought, flashing back to the few times he had visited as a kid with his father.

Chapter 13 – Follow the Data

When he walked through the entrance to CAMPO that afternoon, Kevin was relieved to discover that the beeper had remained silent in his absence. He wanted to be there when it all went down, whatever it was. But it was still a waiting game.

Now it was mid-morning Friday and the beeper was back in his pocket where it belonged. Even though Kevin had developed a full-blown nervous tic around rubbing its smooth surface, he still couldn't make it go off. Instead, he was at his desk, munching on a Twizzler and typing up notes from his visit downtown.

Rafiq leaned over and pointed at the candy. "Those things are gonna rot you from the inside. They're full of red dye that's linked to low sperm count, Alzheimer's and fuck knows what else."

"Thank-you, Doctor Fauci." But Kevin looked at the last bite of the rubbery red braid in his hand, thinking it had been his mother's favorite for years. He tossed it in the bin, groaning.

The desk phone rang, its mechanical chime like a blast from the past. He picked it up, absently, while he finished typing in scribbled notes. "Conley speaking."

"You're not going to believe this. I went back to Starbucks yesterday and there he was again – that smooth operator Carmelo Jones. Great lead on the name by the way…" A moment in, Kevin realized that he hadn't really been listening.

"Whoa, slow down. Larry?" he asked, shifting his attention to catch up with the flow of words.

"Yeah, yeah, it's me, who else? Anyway, Carmelo came into the Starbucks, and holy smokes, charmed his way into another gift card transaction. I spoke to the manager and persuaded her to let me see the transaction record. It wasn't hard once I let her know I thought a customer was scamming her store. I got the P-card number – it wasn't the one that had been issued to Jones. It belonged to another admin in the central office. The Starbucks lady also showed me the data from the day we were there together – same thing – it wasn't even his card. Anyway, I pulled the records for his whole department, and I think he's set himself up as the office gopher, helping with everyone's errands and scut work, anticipating that they wouldn't pay much attention to the charges. And the dude was right about that: I've identified over five thousand dollars of suspicious activity. He's got his own little side gig turning over gift cards for fun and profit."

"Larry, that's wild. Why didn't the financial manager catch it?"

"He works in college admissions – they tend to have lots of small charges for little events and freebies that they hand out to visiting families. Carmelo was good at keeping the values below the radar."

"You've got a real knack for stakeouts. How'd you know he'd be back?" Kevin scribbled on his note pad.

"I didn't. I went in for my normal coffee and saw the same barista on duty, so I figured I'd sit there and read my emails in case anything interesting happened. And voila! I think if we can catch him in the act one more time, we've got him.

"I have a couple free hours this afternoon," Kevin said. "I can tail him; see what happens."

"That would be great! Today is probably a long

shot, but if you get lucky, I think we have enough evidence to terminate this guy."

Kevin glanced at his calendar and confirmed that he had an open slot from two to four. "I'm on it," he said.

"Thanks man, we're closing in!" Kevin was just about to hang up when Larry said, "Oh wait, I almost forgot. I got that other data you asked for, about that super, Dory Johnson."

Kevin stopped chewing. "Hit me," he said, feeling the adrenaline start to tingle down his spine.

Larry replied, "So, there's a pretty heavy pattern of MRA's"

"Whats?" asked Kevin.

"MRAs – missing receipt authorizations. It's a form that people use when they want to get reimbursed for an expense, but they've lost the receipt. It's usually legit: people do lose stuff occasionally, which is why the form exists. But a pattern of frequent use can be a red flag. Anyway, like I said, Johnson has a heavy pattern. And then she also submitted a bunch of expense reports WITH receipts, for identical amounts. So, I suspect double-dipping on the purchasing reimbursements. Some of these purchases, there's no reason why they weren't direct-billed in the first place. She's noncompliant with procurement policy. Anyway, seeing the pattern I spent a little extra time pulling records on some other building supers, you know, just to see if her patterns are unusual. Sometimes, with people who are not tech savvy, it can just be a training issue. We keep implementing these new computer systems to support purchasing, and it's a tough transition for some of the buildings folks who worked their way up from custodial roles. I mean, they're not exactly Steve Jobs."

Larry was really warming to his subject, but Kevin wasn't interested in the technical arcana of financial transactions policy. He just wanted to know: was Dory Johnson an embezzler?

"You think she's crooked?"

"I think there's something there," Larry replied. "I'm going to send you some docs in interoffice mail. I know it's old-fashioned, printing it out on paper and all, but when I use the highlighter and tape flags, the patterns really stand out. I mean, it's striking. Really made me curious about why you're putting the bead on her."

"I can't say, friend. But I appreciate the data – it's going to help a great deal."

"OK, fair enough. We can talk again when you see the report, and I want to check a few other things on my end too. But as I said, aside from this one other building super, Deacon, she's way out of line."

"Wait a second, did you say Deacon?" A fresh jolt of adrenaline pulsed through Kevin.

"Yeah, he's the super in Masterman over on East Campus. Also a big user of MRAs. But I don't want to distract you. I think there's enough data on Johnson to support whatever suspicions you have. I think you're really onto something there."

Kevin remembered to ask about the phone records.

"I made that request through IT; nothing yet. I'll call you when it comes in. And let me know how things go tailing Carmelo Jones today."

"Will do," said Kevin, wrapping up the call.

Kevin hung up the phone and turned to an investigator's best friend, Google search. He clicked on the maker space and found the Who We Are section. He found the full names of Sheila's friends, the "board of advisors" he had met the other night. The Deacon and the others. He Googled them. He checked the university directory and confirmed that The Deacon and Lloyd Deacon, superintendent of Masterman Hall on East Campus, were one and the same. He told himself he wouldn't be doing this if Larry hadn't brought it up. He thought of his old girlfriend Heather and his sworn vow not to dig up dirt on friends.

He tried to bring himself back to the case, back to the real work. With Larry's new information, he decided to check whether Dory Johnson had a criminal record. She was clean. Then he checked Deacon and the others. He checked Sheila herself – she was also clean. But the others…

With each click, his gut felt queasier. He wondered if his face had gone pale; he knew he was sitting unnaturally still. He tried to shake off a growing sensation of moral cloudiness. This was all public information and investigating suspicious activity at the university was his job. And there was the unexpected connection between Dory's M.O. and Deacon's activity, which had just dropped into his lap. When they met, why hadn't Deacon mentioned that he worked at the university? It would have been so natural. At some level, Kevin was obligated to check it out. Right?

And the record wasn't clean. Deacon had a misdemeanor charge twenty years ago, apparently from a bar fight. One of the snarky lesbians had a DUI and a drunk and disorderly – only a few years old. Kevin thought back to the diet cokes that half of them were drinking that night. Maybe they'd turned their lives around. But given Deacon's pattern of shady financial transactions? Maybe not. He wondered if he should ask Larry for the dates on Deacon's MRAs. Or maybe he should remember his own rules and walk away from this thread. He heard the echo of his father's voice, repeating another piece of cop's wisdom: *the world is full of coincidences. You need two points of connection to make it matter.* This thing with Deacon was probably just a coincidence. He should shake it off.

He closed the tabs he'd left open and rolled his chair away from the screen. Standing up to stretch, on his way to the water cooler, he reminded himself that Larry's real find was the info about Dory. He needed to write it up; inform Mulally and Hamish that it might be a lead. If he got all that done quickly, he'd still have time to return

Larry's favor and tail Carmelo Jones this afternoon.

Around four-thirty, Kevin felt the chill of the
quad's waning light as he sat on a bench with a clear sight
line to the main entrance of Harker Hall. He was
practicing nonchalance, smoking a cigarette, and scrolling
through his phone as he listened to the door open and
close. He'd been sitting there about forty-five minutes and
had memorized the particular *scratch* and *thunk* the door
emitted when it was opened from the inside. There was no
sign of Carmelo Jones yet. He shifted his position and
stretched. It was the first time he'd felt idle that week;
things had really been popping on multiple fronts. There
was nothing like a murder to amp up the workload in a
police department.

A distant *thunk* pulled his attention back to
Harker. Bingo. There was Carmelo Jones, heading toward
the nearest gate and the shopping area beyond. Kevin
checked his watch, then rose and followed at a leisurely
pace. They moved toward Staples – office supplies. Kevin
followed Carmelo into the store, noting the copy center in
the corner, not quite close enough to observe the bank of
checkout cashiers. There were only two registers open at
the front of the store. Carmelo wandered briefly among
the pens and pencils before pausing at a large rack of gift
cards from all the big-box chain stores. Jesus, Kevin
thought. He'd never paid much attention to these displays,
but now that he knew more about their nefarious
potential, he realized he'd been seeing them all over town.
It was like catnip for small-time hustlers.

Carmelo picked four cards off the rack and
stepped into the checkout line. Kevin perused a display of
ballpoint pens, and as soon as another customer got in line
behind Carmelo, Kevin snatched up a pack of pens and
moved in behind them. When Carmelo reached the
register and began his transaction, Kevin surreptitiously
snapped a cell photo. He could see the telltale splash of

gold when Carmelo handed over his university purchasing card. This time, the cashier didn't bat an eye. She just processed the payment and handed over the receipt, asking, "Do you need a bag?" in the bored manner of cashiers everywhere. Carmelo said, "No thanks," took the receipt, and left the store.

Chapter 14 - Missed Date

The Packers scored; the bar erupted. There were two minutes left in the second quarter; Kevin had twenty bucks riding on the split. If they could hold on to the lead, he would get the money and the bragging rights. Feeling confident, he ordered another round for himself and Rafiq, sitting on his left at the wide oak counter. It was Sunday afternoon. They were two beers in and enjoying the mid-afternoon buzz. It was the first time that week that Kevin hadn't been thinking about work. When Rafiq had suggested on Friday that they meet up at the pub to watch the game, Kevin enthusiastically agreed. "Hell, yeah." Looking around the pub now – three-quarters full, mostly guys just hanging out, eating burgers at the bar and enjoying the game, he repeated to himself, "This is exactly what I needed." The bartender set down the beers; Rafiq thanked him with a gentle fist to Kevin's bicep. They raised the icy glasses and tapped them together before taking a quaff. His plan for the rest of the day was to grab an Uber home after the game and take a nap. When the whistle blew, second down and still ten yards to go, he glanced down at his phone and noticed a message had come in. It said Sheila.

He tipped the phone up to read the text. *You coming?*

Shit. He'd forgotten all about the date they had made two weeks ago, to set up easels together in that spot by the river. She was probably already there waiting for him, having lugged her gear to the spot they'd picked out. There was no way he could make it across town in time. And did he really want to leave the cold beer and the camaraderie of the warm barroom?

He cursed his forgetfulness, and almost immediately tried to justify it by tossing some blame in her direction as well. They had scheduled this for two weeks away because she had been traveling last weekend, visiting family out of state. Unlike other women he had dated, she hadn't sent him any reminder messages. She'd just assumed that he would show up as agreed. He didn't want to acknowledge the gaffe was on him.

"What's up, man?" Rafiq asked.

"Nothing, man. Just something I forgot to do."

At that moment, the Packers intercepted and started running the ball back toward the endzone. It was one of those miraculous plays, the kind of thing that only happens in sport. The sheer surprise sent the room into another loud burst of whoops and groans. After the replay, once they were sure there was no flag, Rafiq slapped a twenty on the bar, saying, "No fucking way!"

Kevin picked up the cash and stuffed it in his pocket. "Before you figure out how to weasel out..." he laughed. He was trying to figure out how to reply to that text.

Something came up at work — sorry I forgot to let you know. I'll call you later.

It seemed kinder and easier to lie than to admit that he straight-up forgot. He must have sighed as he put the phone down on the bar, because Rafiq turned quizzically to glance at the screen.

"Everything OK?" he asked again.

"I was supposed to meet someone today; I totally spaced on it."

"Judging from how vague you are being, I'm guessing it's a lady." Rafiq leaned into the word *lady*.

"Yeah. Sheila. We've gone out a couple of times.

She's good – I can't believe I forgot. She didn't remind me, and I just…I'm an idiot." Elbows on the bar, Kevin shook his head into his hands.

"Well, she's not your dentist so she isn't required to send you appointment reminders," Rafiq ribbed him. "Maybe this means you don't like her that much."

Kevin found himself objecting right away. "No, it's not that. She's cool. I mean, I'm not the 'love at first sight' type but she's nice. She's fun. We have a good time together."

Rafiq's eyes were trained on the game. He said, "Well, apologize and think of some way to make it up to her. If it's meant to be, it will work out. If not…" Rafiq shrugged.

"Easy for you to say; typical married guy," Kevin said. "It's tough out here being single."

Both men kept their eyes trained on the game. Then Rafiq turned back to Kevin.

"I'm not gonna pull some macho BS and say I miss the dating life. Every night I fall asleep next to Marie is a good night. Even if the house does smell like baby poo. Still worth it." Rafiq turned back to the big screen with a little, true smile that reminded Kevin why they were friends. "Apologize and do better next time."

Kevin nodded. Looking back at the game, his mind wandered along the question: why did he forget? The busy week, his preoccupation with the murder investigation and working with Hamish and the city cops, the fact that he had multiple cases open. He liked Sheila; she was easy to talk to and friendly. He sincerely hoped to have sex with her again. A sour lurch in his gut reminded him of the data he'd seen about Deacon and the others. Was he subconsciously avoiding her? That felt closer to the truth. He took another swig of the beer, warming on the bar in front of him.

His phone lit up again.

That sucks, she wrote.

139

Did she mean for him or for her? Kevin typed in a reply immediately.

I'm really sorry I didn't let you know. I'll make it up to you. Gotta run. He watched the screen for the telltale three dots of a reply, but he got nothing.

Kevin figured she probably went ahead with the painting. That seemed like what she would do, even if she was feeling lonely and peeved. He thought of the extra gear she had probably lugged over to accommodate two people working together. He glanced at the windows behind him and noticed for the first time that it was one of those rare mild, springlike days with low sun flashing off the changing leaves. It would be beautiful down by the river today. For a minute, he thought about changing course and heading down there. On the one hand, it felt like a romantic gesture and a speedy recovery from his mistake. On the other hand, with beer on his breath and a thirty-minute drive between them, did it really make sense? Would it make his white lie even more obvious?

Kevin stayed for the rest of the game, but the fun had gone out of it. When Rafiq won back his twenty in the last quarter, Kevin chalked it up to karma.

Chapter 15 - The Etching

Monday morning, Kevin was back at his desk. The interoffice envelope from Larry had just arrived, and Kevin was trying to puzzle through the rows of transaction data. As promised, the dense printout was highlighted and adorned with post-its scribbled with arrows, exclamations points and notes like "same vendor" and "dupe amount." Draining a last swig of cold coffee, he was just starting to follow Larry's logic when a familiar-looking guy walked in and paused uncertainly. Dressed in a university logo "Facilities" polo shirt and black work pants, he seemed to get his bearings when he saw Kevin.

"Hello, Officer," he said, stepping forward and holding out his hand to shake. "I'm Reinaldo Reyes, cleaning supervisor. Do you remember me?"

Kevin searched his mind as they shook; he wasn't sure yet how he knew the guy but he didn't want it to show on his face.

Reinaldo continued, "Listen, I want to tell you, my crew just sent a painting over to the museum. We found it cleaning out a student apartment. But then I recognized it from a different spot. Waverly Hall. I remember that was where you had a theft."

It took Kevin a minute to catch up, but Reyes' reference to "his crew" snapped his memory back in place – this was the guy that Dory had implicated in the art theft before it became a murder investigation. "You found a painting and sent it over to the museum?"

"Yeah, black and white, lots of lines. Very unusual to find real-looking art in these student apartments. And I'm thinking, *I know this picture*! On the back, we find a museum sticker. So I bring it over there yesterday. And then I remember why I knew it. It was in the fancy apartment in Waverly Hall. The one you asked about."

Kevin stomach turned over. "Reinaldo, this is very good news. I'm impressed by your memory! I appreciate your coming by. This could be important; thank you, really, thanks very much."

He pulled up the image of the artwork that he had saved on his phone and showed it to Reinaldo.

"Yes, that's the one," Reinaldo confirmed happily. Kevin took down the rest of the information: the location of the student apartment, the date they had found it, and exactly when it had been returned to the museum. As he walked Reinaldo to the door, thanking him again, he could still feel the nervous, jangly rush of adrenaline.

This could be the clue that broke the whole case open. He might be closing in on the truth – the feeling made him want to rush forward but at the same time do everything with slow deliberation. First step: find out who was living in that apartment.

He called Residential Life. Within moments, he had the three names on the lease and he already knew that only one mattered. Amanda Herring. Before calling her, he needed to coordinate with the city cops. That would take a bit of time, so for now he decided to go see the piece. He didn't have many excuses to look at art while on the job, and he could corroborate Reinaldo's story by speaking with the curator. Looking back through his notes for her name, he came upon the sketch he'd made when they spoke on the phone. Artemis Johns. He called and made an appointment for that afternoon. On an impulse, he texted Jason to come along. The kid would enjoy it, and his weird knowledge of etchings might be useful.

Around three o'clock, he walked through the heavy copper-clad doors of the museum and found Jason waiting inside, head bent over his phone, oblivious to the soaring, sun-filled atrium above. Kevin loved this space, and as he took in the sweep of marble floor connecting the ticket window, the coat room, the coffee shop and the entries to the galleries on three sides, he wondered why he didn't come in more often. Especially when he saw someone who had to be Artemis Johns walking briskly toward them like a superhero in low heels and an asymmetric black cape. Kevin felt a familiar jolt – she was nothing like the Carmen Sandiego type he'd imagined, but striking in a whole different way, with a mass of tumbling dark hair and a dancer's grace concealed under her flowing clothes. She reached out a pale hand in greeting, and it was all Kevin could do to remember his own name, then introduce Jason as a student whose knowledge of etchings had been helpful in the case. Jason took the compliment in stride, and reached out confidently to shake hands, saying, "It's a pleasure to meet you, Ms. Johns."

As she led them to a concealed staircase and up to a private workshop on the second floor, she described how Reinaldo had appeared with the picture the day before. Apologizing for not having called Kevin immediately, she said she had been distracted and delighted by the unusual interruption to her cataloging work.

They had reached a pure white worktable. Reaching down, she pulled the framed picture from a long, narrow slot where it had been resting on end, and placed it flat on the bright surface. The three of them huddled over it together. After all these weeks, Kevin's heart was beating faster just seeing the actual piece, a rather unassuming scratchy black and white image.

"This whole situation is so unusual," she said, pushing her glasses further up the bridge of her nose. "But if seeing the piece can be helpful to your investigation, I'm happy to accommodate. Truly, we're just happy that it was recovered. It was signed out to Waverly Hall five years ago and was just coming due to be returned. Perhaps swapped out for something different."

"Why?" Kevin asked, straightening from the table as they spoke. Jason remained fully absorbed in the etching, his nose just a few inches above the glass.

"Why swap it out?" she responded. "People like art, and we try to keep their environment fresh. There is a theory that if a picture stays on the wall too long, we will stop seeing its beauty." She said this as though touched by the tragedy of overlooked art, sympathetically stroking the edge of the frame. Kevin was charmed but managed to stay on track.

"No, I mean why does the museum let people 'sign out' valuable artworks? Isn't that risky?"

"Ah. It's not unusual for lesser works to be placed around campus – usually in the grander ceremonial spaces or the offices of senior people – deans, chancellors, that sort of thing. It reinforces the image of the whole university as an intellectual oasis dedicated to the arts and sciences. The apartment in Waverly is used for visiting dignitaries and faculty we're trying to recruit, so it's a prime location. We are generally happy for the works to be seen. We are fortunate to have a large collection – larger than what we can display within the walls of the museum. Anyway, I am pleased to see the piece hasn't deteriorated. And what a relief that it wasn't stolen after all – as far as we know, it never left university property."

"How can you tell it hasn't deteriorated?" Jason asked.

"To be honest, mostly from the condition of the frame and matting. I am not an expert on etchings…but you can see that the frame has not been disturbed…the work hasn't been removed in years." As she spoke, she turned the piece over on the table and pointed to the dust and grime on the tiny tacks holding the frame and mounting together. "There are no telltale dings or scratches, no extra tack holes or evidence of prying. So I think it's safe to assume that the piece has not been disturbed. And given that it was carefully preserved with acid-free paper and UV-resistant glass, we can assume that the aging process is also well-managed."

As she turned the piece back over, facing up, Jason removed his backpack and rummaged inside, pulling out a magnifier. "Okay if I use this?" he asked.

Lifting her brows, she said, "By all means. Tell me what you see."

He leaned even further in. "It's a good piece. The printing is very fine. There was a traveling exhibit a few years back on 18th century etchings – I saw it in New York at the Met. This artist, Joseph Marie Vien, was featured. The theme of the exhibit was that, around that time in France, lots of painters experimented with etching techniques, trying to free themselves from the formal constraints of painting in oils."

"Etchings are out of fashion today," she said. "People like color. We have a good-sized collection, but it hasn't been properly studied or catalogued."

Jason remained hunched over the work, squinting through his glass.

"You can see the influence of oil technique in the way he places his lines, like layering paint," he said.

She pulled a second magnifier from a drawer below the table's surface and lowered her head to peer at the piece alongside Jason. From Kevin's position, their dark heads nearly merged as they concentrated together.

"There, for example," Jason said, gesturing to a corner where the artist had depicted a woven basket of grapes in the grass; she nodded. "This print is better than the one they had in the exhibit."

Artemis stood. "A print from this series was in an exhibit at the Met?"

Jason blinked. "Yeah. I remember it because my dad always likes that bacchanal-type shit. Oh, sorry, I mean stuff."

Kevin stood quietly, smiling as he looked from student to curator and back.

"What year are you?" she asked.

"First Year."

"Hmm. Well, Jason. Once again, I am gobsmacked by one of our students. You and I should talk. We could use someone like you around here. It sounds like our assessment of the importance of this part of the collection is a little out-of-date." Jason gave a lop-sided smile.

"And how did you become involved in a CAMPO investigation?" she asked.

"Funny story…" Kevin started to reply.

Jason jumped in. "Detective Conley and I both take the same figure drawing class, in night school. He's a hook lefty, but he does pretty well in spite of that. Last week the model was a golden retriever, and Kevin's drawing was the best in the class."

Artemis' lips blossomed into a slow smile at Jason, which still played on her face as she turned toward Kevin. "Indeed? Like best in show, perhaps?" she said.

Jason laughed. "Oh I get it…like a dog show. That's good."

"This day is getting more and more surprising," said Artemis warmly.

Kevin could feel himself blushing, but his awkwardness was offset by a surprising, almost paternal pride in Jason's precocious knowledge. "Well, listen," he interjected. "I think my work is done here. I'm glad to see the piece, and to hear your confirmation that it hasn't been harmed in its travels. I'll move along and leave the art to the experts. Thank you for your time, and I'm glad the etching found its way back home."

"Yes, and what a relief that now I won't have to

file that insurance claim," she shuddered at the idea.

Kevin laughed, "Amen to that – less paperwork is always a good thing."

They shook hands again, her graceful fingers disappearing into his. He was careful not to squeeze too hard.

"See you next week, Jason," he said as he backed out of the room, to the backs of their two heads already bent together again over the picture. He walked around to the main staircase and descended the wide terrazzo steps slowly, soaking in the warm sunlight streaming through the atrium glass, gazing at the crisp shadows cast by the armature of the skylight, alive to the sensation of being surrounded by people who made and appreciated art, and people who dedicated their lives to understanding artistic expression in its many forms. It was one of those moments when he really loved the university; when it felt like a wondrous prism, exactly as soaring and profound as it aspired to be.

Kevin smoked a cigarette as he walked slowly back to headquarters. He knew his next step and was pondering how to approach it. An image of a magician pulling a long string of knotted scarves from his sleeve came to mind. An investigation was like that - he needed to keep pulling each scarf, smoothly and gently, not knowing when it would reach the end, careful not to disturb the knots holding the story together.

Around four p.m., as the late fall sky began to darken and with Hamish from the city force listening in, he called the cell number listed on Amanda Herring's lease document. He introduced himself, and mentioned that his colleague, Detective Hamish, was also on the line. She remembered him, and before he could say why he was calling, she icily stated that she was no longer a student.

"Oh," Kevin said, "then I guess congratulations are in order."

"For what?"

"Graduating – completing your degree."

She snorted.

"You said you're not a student anymore. Did you not graduate?"

"I transferred. I'll finish my degree at State," she said flatly.

That surprising news hit Kevin like a snag, a bit of resistance in the fabric. He slowed down, pulling the thread even more gently. Something was wrong. Transferring to State was generally a big step down, so the decision begged for an explanation. But he needed to stay focused on the reason for his call.

"This actually has to do with some artwork that was found in the apartment after you moved out. It was a rather valuable piece – part of the university museum collection. Your roommates told me it was yours." He was bluffing, but it worked.

She replied, "Well, it wasn't really *mine*. As you point out it belongs to the university. It was given to me because I admired it, with the understanding that I would leave it on campus after graduation."

"Given to you by whom?"

"Why does it matter?" Her voice remained flat, but he was impressed again by how guileless she seemed. He remembered noticing that the first time they had met.

"Well, it was on display, signed out to a particular location, so whoever moved it really didn't have the authority to do so."

Silence.

"I wonder if it was a gift from James Fensbridge?"

More silence. Kevin tried to interpret the quality of it. "Are you still there?"

"Look," she said. "This whole thing has been a big mistake. You found the painting; what's the big deal?"

"It may be part of something bigger. Tell me, was it Professor Fensbridge?"

This time, she paused for two full beats. Kevin waited, then heard an audible sigh. When she spoke next, there was a catch in her voice.

"We had a relationship; it's over now."

"Was this relationship part of the reason you transferred?" Kevin wanted her to keep talking.

"It got...complicated and awkward. He is, as you know, an important person in the political science department."

"Did he hurt you in some way?"

"I'm not a child! I mean, I knew he was married, but he said it was for convenience. I didn't realize he was also fucking his research assistant. And the coauthor on his last monograph. I was just a naïve fool. Oldest, most banal story ever." She sounded angry, petulant, humiliated.

"Amanda. I'm sorry this happened to you. Do you want to talk about it?"

"GOD! With you? When you are simultaneously accusing me of being some kind of idiot art thief? Oh, this is rich. What a fucked-up place."

"Amanda, I'm not accusing you of anything. I'm just doing my job and trying to do it thoroughly. This is the second time your name has come up in my investigation."

"Like I told you before, I don't know anything. And I don't even know what your bloody 'investigation' is about, so how could I possibly help?" Her voice rose as she refocused her anger at Kevin.

"OK. OK." Kevin wanted to calm her. "Let's switch gears for a second. You have told me something that is outside the bounds of an ethical relationship between a faculty member and a student. Forget the other stuff – I am asking you if he hurt you in some way. That is my main concern right now."

"No, this is no Title IX bullshit. It was a purely consensual thing – Jesus, if anything, I pursued him. Like I said, it was stupid."

Kevin wasn't sure what to say next. He had a hunch that she was not involved in the crime, but he wasn't sure his silent colleague from the city force would see it that way. He had to admit the fact that she had moved out of town in the middle of the term looked suspicious.

"All right. But if you ever need to talk to someone about James Fensbridge's actions, I can connect you with someone who is trained to deal with this type of situation," Kevin was stalling.

"Thanks, but no thanks." The flatness had returned to her voice.

"Regarding my investigation, can you tell me what you were doing in Waverly 12C?"

She snorted again. "I think it's pretty obvious. And I have nothing more to say."

"Okay, Amanda. I appreciate your time. I may call again."

"Please don't." She hung up.

"Fuckin' A," said Hamish. "I'll call you back on a clean line."

Kevin was almost shocked to hear his voice; then the phone went dead. Fucking A was right. When he picked up his ringing line a second later, Hamish jumped in.

"You've gotta follow up on that harassment shit. It might motivate her to talk."

"I don't think she knows anything," said Kevin. "And there's technically no harassment unless she says there is."

"I give you eighty-to-one odds. He's guilty as fuck. Banging his secretary? That's real 1950s shit. You still have secretaries over there?" Hamish sucked in his teeth, three short noisy sucks. "Lucky bastards. Wish I had a secretary to do my paperwork, if you know what I mean. I bet the dead girl was another girlfriend."

Kevin flashed back to the way his father used to talk with his buddies at work – the profane banter, the assumed camaraderie underlying dumb, careless bro-code stereotypes. The warp speed at which Hamish was ready to leap to judgment was unnerving. When Kevin was a boy and his father had seemed all-knowing, this kind of macho stuff had been exciting. Now it was twenty years later, and it felt childish. Churlish, and not worthy. A woman was dead – he felt like she deserved more than being reduced to a sexist stereotype.

"One step at a time," Kevin said. "Let's just keep following the leads."

"She might not know anything, but her boyfriend is the one. We need to nail him."

Kevin wasn't so sure, but he didn't see much upside in arguing. He had said his piece – they would follow the thread and uncover the truth, step by step.

Driving home that night, still mulling over the unexpected news from Amanda Herring, and Hamish's casually cruel response, Kevin decided to swing over to Glenhurst to see his mother. It had been three weeks. Thinking about his father that afternoon had reminded him that he was due for a visit. He followed his usual routine – parking lot, change of shoes and jacket, try to look less like a cop and more like her son. He brought in his sketchpad to pass the time.

"Hello, Officer," she greeted him from her recliner. "You know, I haven't seen my husband in a while. Maybe you know him. Frank Conley. He's left me here, I'm not sure why. Sometimes he acts like a big shot."

"Ma!" Kevin said. "It's me, Kevin, your son. Dad died five years ago, remember?" He sat on the edge of her bed, facing her from his usual angle.

She looked at him steadily, as if deciding whether to believe him or not. Her narrow lips quivered with the effort. Kevin allowed himself to hope. A long moment passed, then another. She looked toward the window, then returned her gaze to his face.

"Maybe you know my husband, Frank," she said. "I think he may have gone off with one of those girls he's been running around with. And now he's locked me in this place." Her eyes were wet. When she blinked, identical tears broke free of each eye and clung to the lower frames of her glasses.

Kevin sat down and reached for her hand. She pulled away and lifted a wad of tissue to her cheek.

"Ma…" he said.

"Shhh…." she replied. And they sat like that for twenty minutes, Kevin listening to the institutional sounds of the women working out at the desk and the other residents in the distance. He started to tell her about a show he had seen on TV, but again she interjected. "Shhhh…" He sat back and pulled out his sketchpad. He started to rough out the slope of her shoulders and was quickly absorbed in the task.

He was startled when she suddenly said, "Kevin? You're here. Oh, I've missed you, Kevin."

He looked up in shock, stammering, "Yeah, it's me. I'm here."

"It's so good to see you; I love to see you drawing, just like when you were a little boy. You could go so deep, almost like in a trance, when you were drawing."

He reached for her hand, buoyant, and she let him take hold.

"I love you, Ma. Things are gonna be okay." She smiled into his eyes, like she was really there.

"Such a smart, sensitive kid. Nothing like your father. You were so curious about the world. Animals, people, places. What a sweetie you were," she said, still smiling.

"You were good to me, Ma," Kevin said. She looked back toward the window. Her grip gradually loosened in his, but he felt a kind of peace that had eluded him for months. Just a glimpse, just a moment that she knew him. He kept watching her face and almost felt that he could see her clarity slip away, replaced by milky confusion.

When he rose to leave, he patted her shoulder. Feeling her stiffen, he went no further.

"I'll see you soon, Ma. Take care."

"Officer. When you see my husband, Frank Conley, tell him I hope he rots in hell. Once a cheater, always a cheater."

Minutes later, Kevin sat in his car in the dark parking lot, composing himself for the drive home. He wanted to cling to the moment of peace and connection between them, when she had seemed to see both her child and the man he had become. He knew it wouldn't last; he would be plunged back into the more common reality of bottomless frustration and loss over never being able to share with her his victories, worries, someday maybe his own children's progress in life. That was the torture of her situation.

And the bitter things she said about Frank – Kevin couldn't know if they were hallucinations or if they were true. He had always thought his parents had a good marriage. And maybe they had. But now he was thinking about cheaters – about his father, about Fensbridge and Amanda and the murdered girl. About himself, lying to Sheila instead of admitting a small, thoughtless mistake. The world was awash in unsolved mysteries, unreliable memories concealing the truth of the human soul.

Chapter 16 - Interviews: Amanda & Fensbridge

Kevin slapped both palms against his thighs, trying to shock himself into getting up and making the phone call he had just spent two cigarettes trying to avoid. It was Tuesday, mid-afternoon. He was sitting on one of his favorite benches in the quad, facing back toward CAMPO headquarters – it was the closest spot a person could smoke unfettered and still be able to see people coming and going. It had taken two butts to process what the Title IX coordinator had told him that morning and to figure out how the information might advance the murder case. Hamish thought it was "fucking simple," but Kevin was proceeding with caution. Given the sensitivity of the situation, Mulally agreed. This time, Kevin would be alone when he called Amanda. By university guidelines, he could not record the call, so his notes would have to suffice.

Just a couple hours ago, he'd met with Annabeth, the Title IX coordinator assigned to the graduate student population. She was slight and pale, as if she'd been recently been hatched right there in her cramped office. The space had a false coziness, with its pastel tablecloth and throw pillows on the straightback chairs. A rustic quilt hung on the wall. Kevin also noticed the accessible box of Kleenex and the noise machine humming softly on the floor outside her door, its electric cord snaking under the door to a wall plug near his right knee.

There was no denying she was skilled in her role, and they had each engaged in some artful questioning, off the record, with no names involved. What Kevin had learned was that there were three existing records involving Fensbridge and female students, spread over the past four years. The records couldn't be called cases because there were no formal complaints. All were consensual but all had ended badly. None of the stories had been brought to the Title IX office by the student herself; all came from worried girlfriends who were willing to name Fensbridge but not their friend. Annabeth had gone to some trouble as she interviewed these friends to determine that the protagonists were, indeed, three different people. There was nothing on record regarding any university employees, which was unfortunate. They had more leverage in those situations.

Annabeth sighed. "The next one – I really want her to go on record."

"Why does it matter?" he asked.

"If she goes on record, I can pull these other cases to establish a pattern of behavior. It's sort of like pressing charges, but on an ethics violation. He is way outside of bounds, and I can use what we know to nail him – but somebody has to step up."

"That's putting a lot of pressure on one person." Kevin was doubtful, remembering his last conversation with Amanda.

"I know," she nodded. "The students are young and vulnerable, and ironically they tend to overestimate their own agency in these interactions. My hope is that in the long run it's more healing for them to feel like they took command of their own power. But I know it's asking a lot."

There was a pause in the conversation. Kevin noted the paper file she held, tipped up like a poker hand to prevent him from glimpsing inside. He noted the three large filing cabinets in the room – unusual in this digital era. He pictured himself rifling through those files.

Her voice brought him back. "The guy is a ticking time bomb. He's like some kind of throwback, but until I get something more real, the department head isn't willing to take it on. It pisses me off. If you've got something, let's work together to bring this home."

Kevin hesitated; he was trying to stay focused on his own investigation. Ugly as it felt, he had to admit the potential ethics violation was mostly useful as leverage toward solving Tiffany Matthews' murder. And that was way beyond the scope of what Annabeth needed to know.

She pressed on. "What's the first initial of her first name?"

Kevin saw no harm in replying. "A."

Her eyes sparked. "OK then, that proves she is a *fourth* woman, and I presume a graduate student because you are here talking with me." They were both groping in the dark because of the statutory privacy restrictions.

"Look," Annabeth said. "I don't know what else you are investigating – we don't usually have CAMPO involved when there's no assault. But if A were willing to come forward it could make a real difference for the next woman, and the next, etcetera."

So now, here he was, knowing he had to call Amanda but not quite ready to pick up the phone. He was still on that bench, rubbing his hands nervously along the gabardine of his uniform pants. He thought of his father saying, "*Square up, jump in.*" He smiled at the memory of the first time he had heard that one – his father had brought him to swimming lessons when he was about six years old. The next thing his father had said was, "*I'm right here. I'll jump in if you need me. But you won't.*"

Kevin rose from the bench and headed in, not noticing the boys playing hacky sack or the young mother and child throwing breadcrumbs to squirrels as he passed by. *Get ready to jump,* he told himself, as he entered HQ.

He went to the conference room, where he could make the call behind a closed door. He punched in her phone number for a second time, biting his lip in hopes that she would answer. She picked up, with the hesitant, "Hello?" that signified she hadn't recognized the number. As he identified himself, he could feel her waves of irritation. He could almost hear a timer ticking behind her curt voice.

"What now?" she asked. Tick tick tick. He decided to get right to the point.

"What if I told you that you are the fourth student he has had a relationship with?"

There was a long pause on the line. Kevin started to wonder if the call had been dropped.

"Amanda?" He heard her breathe out, a long slow sound, almost a whistle.

"Nope," she said. "No. This is not how this is going to go."

"Excuse me?" Kevin asked.

"You are trying to shame me; to make me feel bad – like a little victim. Are you *blackmailing* me to file a Title IX complaint? What is your sick fascination with this guy?"

"Amanda, I am not blackmailing you. I am trying to understand what happened."

"Yeah, right, for your *investigation*." Her voice oozed with derision. "As I said before, I am a full-grown, human woman with agency and control over my own body. I pursued this relationship because I thought he was sexy as hell. It ended badly, that's all. I am not a victim."

"I hear you, I do. Really," Kevin said. "At the same time, I can't help noticing that he is still here and you have left your program. You won't get the degree you worked so hard for. And, yeah, you made the choice…but to me, the fact that this one professor has had four relationships with students recently - that matters. It's a clear violation of the faculty ethics code. I can't help thinking that you are paying a high price here. Maybe he, I don't know, manipulated you or something?"

"Whatever. What is it you really want to know? Is this all about that dumb shitty painting that was never even stolen?? Why are you obsessed with Fensbridge?"

Of course, he could not tell her about the murder. He hedged again, pushed off-balance by her aggressive stance.

"You're right – this isn't about the etching. But there have been other shady things happening in that apartment, and I'm worried that more women might be at risk."

She snorted. "He may be a colossal disappointment as a human being, but I don't truly think anyone's in *danger*."

"And as you know, it's not even his apartment. But Amanda, you and Fensbridge are the only leads we've got right now, and I need to be thorough. I can't tell you any more than that. And just in case you change your mind, I'm going to text you the contact info for the Title IX office. Just in case. I won't be involved; I won't even know if you call them."

Then came the part Kevin had really been dreading. But he had to ask, to make a clear connection between this relationship and the bizarre evidence in 12C. He had talked it through with Mulally, and they both agreed it might be important.

"Was there anything unusual – kinky – in your relations? Any surprising fetishes or strange acts you, ah, performed together?"

Her voice remained cold as she barked out a short laugh. "Officer, I don't know what might seem kinky to you."

"Like, ah, defecation or urination during the sex act?"

"Gross! This is ridiculous. You really are a sick fuck. Don't call me again." The line went dead.

Well, that went well, Kevin thought. His gut
believed her, though. Her response had been so immediate
and visceral. As he looked at the blank phone screen, he
found himself thinking that a murder case might be
simpler than a Title IX case. There was no he said/she
said. The incontrovertible fact of a dead body could cut
through a lot of human bullshit. He walked across the
office to tell Mulally about the latest dead end.

"Okay," said Mulally, unruffled as usual. "Not
unexpected. We look elsewhere for our poopers."

Kevin chuckled, shaking his head at how pleased
Mulally looked about his little joke.

Mulally said, "I know, but sometimes you gotta
lighten up a little. Let's see how it goes with the man
himself tomorrow."

Mulally had negotiated the time and the setting for
the meeting with Fensbridge. No one wanted a scene near
the professor's office, so they finally agreed that the most
discreet option was to meet at CAMPO headquarters early
in the morning when few people would be in the quad.
Now it was seven am, and Kevin, Mulally and Hamish had
gathered around the table in the same spartan conference
room, nursing bad coffee in chipped gold university mugs.
They all watched the clock, wondering how late he would
be.

Fensbridge strode in, bigger than life, trailing his
open trench coat like wings, ten minutes after the hour.

"You could have sent a simple email update on
those nuisance messages, Chief Mulally. Why am I here?"

Mulally ignored the question. "I think you know
Detective Conley, and this is Detective Hamish from the
city force."

"What's this all about?" Fensbridge loomed over
them, standing tall with his arms folded across his chest.

"Please take a seat. We have a few questions, and if we can keep the answers short and sweet, we can save ourselves a lot of time."

"Am I being accused of something?" He shrugged off his coat and tossed it over an empty chair. He sat down with both feet planted firmly on the floor. Back straight, he shot his cuffs before placing forearms on the table, his hands clasped in front. He trained his gaze on each of the seated men in turn, starting with Hamish and working his way around to Kevin. All three men looked evenly and steadily back at him. They had all been trained in investigation, interrogation, and power dynamics. Kevin's fingers itched to draw the scene, like something from a courtroom drama.

As they had agreed in advance, Kevin took the lead on the questioning. "We want to talk with you about Amanda Herring and a break-in in Waverly Hall, Suite 12C."

"A break-in? I have no idea what you're talking about. This seems like a lot of drama for a trivial matter. I have a seminar to teach in thirty minutes." This was a bluff; there were no classes scheduled on campus before eighty-thirty a.m.

And so it went, neither short nor sweet. Fensbridge admitted to having a relationship with Amanda and repeated his earlier justification about the ethics issue – she was neither a student nor a subordinate during the time of their relationship. It had ended amicably a few weeks ago. He stated that, as far as he knew, her research interests had changed and she had transferred to another school. He admitted that they had used the apartment in Waverly Hall as a meeting place; he smugly said there had been no break-in because in fact he had a key.

"How did you get the key to the apartment," Kevin asked.

"A semester before I joined the faculty, I was here for a month as a visiting fellow. That was where I stayed. I

160

forgot to return the key at the time; later I discovered that it still worked. It proved useful."

"I'll need you to give me that key now," Kevin said.

Fensbridge pulled his keys from his pocket and carefully slid one from the ring, locking eyes with Kevin throughout the maneuver. He laid it gently on the table and pushed it forward with one finger, cocking an eyebrow in disdain. Kevin inspected it, pretending to recognize the etched code KVRQ before slipping into his shirt pocket and returning Fensbridge's gaze.

Hamish asked, "Does your wife know about Amanda and the others?"

"Clever phrasing, Detective." Fensbridge said. "I hardly think that is relevant. But if you must know, no – my wife does not know about Amanda."

"How many times did you go to 12C?" Kevin asked.

"Good lord, man, this questioning is absurd. How would I know?"

"I just think it's strange, knowing the campus as I do, that some nosy super wouldn't have noticed you coming and going in an empty apartment," said Kevin.

"Ah, as it happens, I know that super, Dory Johnson, because I helped her get that job. Her father was my barber. Salt of the earth. I've heard she does an excellent job over there, though we rarely speak." Kevin was stupefied that Fensbridge maintained the confidence and demeanor of a pillar of academia while he made this extraordinary admission.

A moment later, Hamish said, "There's been a murder," and the temperature in the room seemed to drop twenty degrees. Fensbridge's face changed in an instant, looking gray and older. The bags under his eyes grew larger; his cheeks dropped lower. Both detectives could see he was authentically shocked and upset. "Has something happened to Amanda?" He asked. "Dear girl…"

"No," said Kevin. "Someone else. But there's a link to 12C." The professor's face immediately shifted to relief and then moved toward confusion.

"But what does this possibly have to do with me?"

Hamish pointed out, "You have an illicit link to 12C, so you are a person of interest in the murder investigation."

"That's absurd."

"Is it?" Hamish put his own forearms on the table and leaned in hard, mimicking Fensbridge' posture. "You've just admitted that you had an affair with a student, you trespassed on private property, and you're implicated with the super. Sounds suspicious as hell to me."

Fensbridge was silent for two beats longer; this time he didn't have a ready answer.

Until he did.

"There is no truth in what you are suggesting. We won't be discussing this any further without my lawyer present. I will not be threatened in my place of employment."

He rose, picked up his trench, folded it smoothly over his arm, and walked slowly and deliberately out the door. The three other men, still seated, watched as he walked out of the building.

Hamish spoke first. "Jesus. He's guilty as fuck. This is definitely our guy."

Kevin glanced at Mulally, who shook his head almost imperceptibly.

"I'm not so sure," Kevin said. "He's an asshole, but that doesn't make him a murderer. From what we know from Amanda and the other relationships with women, there's no violence or threat in his M.O. There are still a bunch of loose ends."

Mulally started listing, "There's Dory Johnson's dodgy transaction history. There's the other two people who were in the apartment. Who knows what questionable people Tiffany knew from the club scene."

Hamish interrupted, "Yeah, Smitty's chasing down leads at the clubs, but it's slow going. I don't think she made much of an impression. But now we've connected Fensbridge and Johnson. They are in cahoots. When do we get those phone records? This place moves so slow."

Kevin sighed and agreed to follow up, reminding them it would be just a list of numbers called – no information on what people talked about and no mobile phone records unless Hamish ordered them. That was outside university jurisdiction. He thought it was a long shot.

As they talked through their next steps, Hamish focused on tightening the case around Fensbridge. Mulally and Kevin brought up other threads, other possibilities.

Hamish glanced at his watch. "Shit. I've gotta get downtown. I think there's one thing we can agree on: we need that motion sensor to trigger. We need to catch someone in the act."

Mulally nodded, "And after today, if that thing goes off we know it won't be Fensbridge in there."

Chapter 17 – Apologies

Even with everything that had happened that week, Kevin hadn't been able to shake his guilty regret about missing the date with Sheila last Sunday. It was like a bad pop song riffing below the surface of his thoughts – always there, ready to intrude in a spare moment. He still didn't understand why he'd made the gaffe and he knew he wanted to take Rafiq's advice and try again. But with everything starting to pop at work, it wasn't until Thursday that he found a moment to reach out to her. He texted, then followed with a call, using his most ingratiating voice, and leading off with another apology.

"If you didn't want to do it, you should have just said so," she said.

"It wasn't that. I was just busy at work and forgot to let you know. Believe it or not, there's a lot of crime fighting on campus these days. I want to make it up to you: come over on Saturday and I'll cook dinner for you."

"Why?" she asked.

"I don't know. I like you." His words hung in the air. Then he had a sudden flash of insight. "I took your advice – I hung one of my pictures. I want to show you. Plus, I make a pretty good roast chicken. C'mon, it'll be fun."

She hesitated.

"Give me another chance. I promise you I am not

normally a flake. I have plenty of faults, but egregious flakiness is not one of them," he said, trying again with the winning voice.

"OK," she laughed. "Last chance for the caped crusader, on account of all the good crime fighting you've been doing."

Fair enough, he thought, as they rang off. He texted the details to her and got a quick thumbs up. He allowed himself a moment of silent celebration before he realized he would have to make good on his impulsive statement and hang some art. Could he even remember what was stacked in the trunk?

Kevin had a lot of wheels in motion, and again he felt that satisfying sense of positive momentum. They were making steady progress on the murder investigation. Sheila had agreed to give him another chance on Saturday, and tomorrow was the exciting conclusion of the Carmelo Jones saga. The data collection was complete; the trap had been set. First thing tomorrow morning, the final step in the process – exactly as Larry had described it to him weeks ago at Starbucks - was about to go down.

Chapter 18 – Taking down Carmelo Jones

On Friday morning, Kevin dressed in his full officer's uniform. He was "the muscle" after all. He came in early that day, reviewed the duty schedule and checked on the beeper, and headed over to Harker Hall, where he was now standing discreetly around the corner from a conference room on the second floor, waiting for Carmelo Jones.

But nothing ever goes according to plan, and in one of those moments that made Kevin think, "you can't make this stuff up," Carmelo had failed to show up at work that morning. The team had assembled at nine a.m.: Larry Melnick, head of HR Marilyn Burns, and Kevin. They spent an impatient quarter-hour waiting for the perp to appear. Whatever human sympathy they had harbored for him melted away as the minutes ticked by. Word came through at nine-thirty from Carmelo's supervisor that she had called his home number and woke him up – he had stammered that his alarm clock hadn't gone off. He was simply and embarrassingly late for work. The termination team cooled their heels, investing just a bit more of the university's time and money in Carmelo Jones.

He had finally arrived and as soon as the conference room door closed behind him, Kevin stepped forward and positioned himself just outside. Clasping his hands in front of his wide belt, his right forearm perched gently atop the holster cover that held his service revolver, Kevin pictured the conversation happening inside the room. They had thoroughly briefed it beforehand.

Sitting around the polished walnut table, in the gleaming upholstered chairs usually reserved for visitors to the President's Office, Mr. Jones was being read his last rites as an employee of the university. It wouldn't take long. About now, Marilyn would be wrapping up the conversation. "Here's what's going to happen next, Carmelo. A university police officer is waiting outside. You will walk together to your desk, where you will pick up your personal effects, and then he will walk you out of the building. You will leave your keys and your ID with me right now, as well as your purchasing card."

The door opened. Carmelo's preppy confidence had vanished. He ran a shaking hand through his hair, and his eyes darted around the hushed office space, looking for an escape route. As if he could disappear from this potentially criminal situation.

"We'll go straight to your desk to pick up your things," said Kevin. Carmelo led the way, his head pulled into his shoulders. He seemed to shrink a little with every step. Kevin followed a few steps behind. When Carmelo sat down at his cube and reached under the desk for his backpack, Kevin hung back a few feet, standing solidly on both feet, hands remaining clasped in front. Co-workers in neighboring cubes looked up to see Carmelo's ashen face and the uniformed cop hovering nearby and a buzz spread around the area. A young woman in the next cube quietly asked Carmelo if everything was OK. Kevin broke in calmly, "Just your personal effects." Carmelo seemed to understand the drill. He said to the friend, "I'll call you later," before sweeping a few odds and ends into the open top of his backpack.

Kevin held the door for Carmelo, and they walked out together. Once they had crossed the threshold of the building, Kevin led Carmelo, who now seemed like a defenseless boy, to a quiet spot under a tree.

"Carmelo, I'm going to walk you off the campus now. Before we go, I want you to show me your wallet, so that I can confirm there are no more university purchasing cards in your possession." This wasn't part of the script, but Kevin had a hunch and he didn't see any harm in it. Carmelo pulled it out of his pocket and flipped it open. It was a nice wallet, with neat little compartments jammed with plastic cards. There was a goldenrod card right on top, and Kevin could see a university-issued credit card as well, the familiar crest emblazoned on the upper right.

"Please give me those two cards." Carmelo complied. As he slid the first P-card out, another shiny golden surface was revealed. Carmelo glanced up to see if Kevin had noticed. Kevin nodded and gestured "keep them coming" by curling the fingers of his outstretched hand. Kevin collected a total of four P-cards and 2 credit cards before walking Carmelo to the gate.

"Why'd you do it?" Kevin asked. In his experience, this question rarely elicited any real information. Still, he always asked. It was the most interesting question, after all. Carmelo gave him a derisive side-eye and snorted.

"What did you use the money for?" Kevin persisted.

"Dude, this isn't some episode of Law and Order. Fuck off."

Kevin shrugged. One of these days, it was going to work. He nodded at the gate and they walked toward it together.

As Kevin stood under the arch watching Carmelo Jones walk away, he shook his head over the paucity of the punishment. He knew you could trade in gift cards for cash at a central exchange for 75 cents on the dollar. It was trivial, but this discounting was one of the things that really razzed him about this case – Carmelo had taken at least $10,000 – that was what they *knew* about, plus there were these extra cards in his hand. So, conservatively speaking, at 75 cents on the dollar, at least $2500 of university money had simply vaporized. Lost to the middlemen of grift. And that was just this one kid.

Kevin thought about where all that money had come from. He thought about the families trying to scrape together tuition; the government grants that were supposed to support cancer research and instead were supporting this little thoughtless scumbag. He thought about all the dining hall workers and secretaries who could really use a raise – and whose prospects were diminished because of this kind of venal waste in the system. He worked himself into a dark froth of righteous indignation thinking about punks like Carmelo, now crossing the city park back to his apartment, no doubt making up a story about the injustice of his dismissal that would pass muster with his unsuspecting friends. With all the opportunities he had enjoyed, still he decided to dabble in crime and take more. His theft was well over the felony limit of $500, and he was just walking away down the tree-lined street, as if he didn't have a care in the world.

For some reason, the image of Tiffany's friend Alison came, unbidden, into Kevin's mind. He pictured her sitting in Hamish's downtown interrogation room, and the look on her face when she said, *"We didn't know anyone at those fancy places. We were just regular kids."* The contrast between the Carmelo fate, so smooth and supple - and the rough justice meted out to Tiffany Matthews weighed heavily on Kevin. His thoughts arced back to the beeper at HQ, and how stubbornly silent it remained. Would they ever solve the case? At least in the case of Carmelo, a villain had been caught.

Kevin walked over to Larry's office to hand over the additional cards. Larry would track down the people to whom they had been issued and do some transactions research on them. Unless he found something egregious, each of them would get a stern talking-to by Larry and their supervisor. Maybe they would be more careful next time.

But Larry was feeling good. He grinned from ear to ear when Kevin tossed the additional cards on his desk. "Wow, man. That's impressive. We should work together more often."

"I don't know. It makes me kind of sick, watching people walk away with no consequences."

Larry face turned serious. "I know. We review the protocol every couple of years because it starts to get to us, but we always come to the same conclusion. It's better not to tell them how much we think they took, or what the 'real' punishment would be if we pressed charges. It emboldens them; if they are working with others, they share the information and the petty stuff spreads like a virus. We just tell them 'We know what you did,' show enough evidence to get them to fold, ask them to sign the acknowledgement and the NDA, and walk them off campus. If we catch them before the money gets too big, that's best case…because no one just stops on their own.

"You gotta look at the big picture," he continued. "There are thousands of employees here…and a vanishingly small number of bad guys."

"I know, I know," said Kevin. "I tell myself that all the time. I guess you and I have the same occupational hazards."

Larry smiled again. "Look, in the last few weeks, we've put a real dent in the ratio. I've been writing a new training module for financial managers, sort of forensic accounting 101. You should help me with that! You and I are the inhouse experts now…"

"I'm not much of a writer – how would that work?" Kevin asked. As they batted around a few ideas, Kevin's enthusiasm grew. He liked Larry's thinking, that with the right training, they could stamp out a lot of this stuff before it happened – they could reduce both the means and the opportunity.

Checking the clock, Kevin said, "Oh man, I need to get back to HQ."

He rose to leave, just as Larry said, "Hey, by the way, those phone records you wanted came in this morning while we were out. Let's see what you've got."

Kevin came around behind Larry's desk and leaned in while Larry pulled up the file. Together they looked at it – the raw download of calls on Dory's office landline. Larry scrolled down to see the total number of records – it was just a few hundred, starting two years earlier and going up to last week.

Larry observed, "Before cell phones, there would have been way more records…"

There were records for both outgoing and incoming calls. For each record, there was a date, the phone number that had been connected, and the duration of the call. For calls within the university, the record also included the name of the person assigned to that phone number.

"Let's sort by date and look at the most recent ones first."

And there they were…five calls over the past two months with James Fensbridge. So maybe Hamish was right. Kevin noticed Deacon's name on the list as well. Many of the calls were outside the university with no name attached. Kevin needed to get this data to Mulally, and then over to Hamish asap – some of these outside calls could shed light on the case, and maybe Smitty could lend a hand tracking them down.

"Wow. This is fantastic. Email me that file; this is going to be extremely useful," Kevin said.

"You got it. And someday you can tell me what the big mystery is," Larry replied.

Kevin left Larry's office feeling great - belatedly experiencing that little thrill of satisfaction that comes with making a bust. The bonus of fresh leads in the murder case amplified his frisson of well-being. He was flattered by the prospect of becoming an "inhouse expert" who could train financial managers in forensic accounting. He crossed the quad, noting its beautiful symmetry as he crossed on the diagonal toward CAMPO headquarters. The sky was a true cerulean blue, like it had been squeezed from a new tube of oil paint. And he had a date for Saturday night.

Chapter 19 - Last Date

The first thing Kevin did on Saturday morning was walk down to his car, parked under the condo, and flip through the art projects that were stored in the trunk. They were in a big stack, taking up the right-hand side of the space. He cleared a spot on the left and started at the top, with the most recent drawings from class and from his last visit to Glenhurst. He considered each piece before flipping it over; as he went deeper in the stack he could barely remember making some of them. Finally, he settled on the charcoal sketch of the dog along with an older gouache landscape from a class three semesters ago. It was colorful; he thought of the curator Artemis Johns saying, "People like color." On an impulse, he also pulled out the small canvas he'd made on their first date. His plan was to run over to the art supply store and pick up a couple of cheap frames, some matting and picture hangers. He already owned a hammer.

Around six, everything was in place. The gouache looked pretty sharp over the couch, and the drawing of the dog was in the hallway leading toward his bedroom. He had propped the little Art Barn canvas on the counter between the kitchen and dining space. Sheila was set to arrive any minute. Kevin was roasting a chicken. He'd made a green salad and bought some wine and cookies for dessert.

Sheila arrived, a little breathless from climbing the stairs, carrying wine and pastries. They exchanged a chaste kiss on the cheek. "Welcome, come on in," he said, then asked her to choose some music while he poured her a glass of wine. While she perused her playlists for inspiration, Kevin tucked away the cookies he had bought, leaving her pastries on the counter. He apologized again for missing their date, offering the explanation that he was preoccupied with a big case right now; that it was bigger than a normal case and it was stressful because they were coordinating with the city cops. She barely raised her eyes from scanning the playlists. Kevin realized that Sheila didn't know enough about police work to be impressed by his partnership with the city.

Looking around the place through her eyes, Kevin noticed the condo seemed pretty bare. As if reading his mind, she said, "Nice place you've got here. Minimalist". She had stopped in front of the couch, looking at the gouache as she sipped her wine. "Did you put these up just for me?"

"Busted," he replied.

"You do good work – where's the rest of it?"

"Still in my trunk," he laughed. "But I owe you a big thanks – it was fun going through the stack and seeing what was there. Some terrible stuff, some already forgotten, and a couple of good ones. The biggest surprise was how many there were in there – made me realize I've produced a lot of work in the last few years."

"How long before dinner is ready? I'd like to see what's in your trunk."

Kevin couldn't resist; her playful tone sounded like an invitation. He stepped close behind her and lifted her hair from her shoulders to kiss the nape of her neck.

"That's what all the girls say," he murmured. She turned, giggling, into a full embrace. They kissed for a while, slowly moving toward the hallway to his bedroom. They agreed dinner could wait; Kevin switched off the oven as he passed by.

The sex was better than the first time; wasn't that generally true? Afterward, they got half-dressed and ate ravenously with their fingers. She looked perfectly at home with her loose curls, wearing one of his T-shirts over her panties. Kevin, bare-chested, had pulled on a pair of gym shorts.

"Tell me something about yourself," Sheila asked.

"There isn't much to tell," he replied. "Grew up here, father was a cop, always wanted to follow in his footsteps. I'm working on my MFA at the university, going to night school."

"Your father's retired now? You said he *was* a cop. And what about your mom?"

"He died several years ago. My mom has early Alzheimer's and lives in assisted living."

"I'm sorry," she said. "That's tough."

Kevin nodded, wanting to turn the conversation back to her. "Thanks. How about you?"

"Oh, you know much more than that about me," she countered. "Tell me about a wild case at work."

Kevin told her about the admirable Ted Sevilla, the scrawny hero of the false fire alarm in the dorm weeks ago - clinging to the smoke alarm in his shaving cream-soaked boxers. It was a good story, the kind of thing people expect from a campus cop. She loved it, laughing heartily at the image.

But Kevin wanted her to know that his job was real, that it wasn't all fun and games and adolescent hijinks, so as they opened the second bottle of wine, he told her about the embezzlement work he was doing with internal audit. He felt disloyal talking about it; he wanted people to think well of the university. He always hated to crush their idealistic image that everything on the inside was heady, utopian stuff – great minds focused only on big thoughts. In his experience, there are saints and sinners peppered everywhere. He talked about the petty thieves, emphasizing that the percentages were lower than most other large organizations. He told her that just that week, they had terminated a young guy.

"I guess these are just 'crimes of opportunity,'" he said. "People justify their actions by talking about the university's large endowment or the football coach's huge salary. But they know they're doing something wrong. That's the downside of the kind of work I do – I spend a lot of time with the bad guys."

The mood in the room had darkened along with the sky; Kevin wanted to lighten it up, and Sheila helped by saying, "I think most people are good."

Kevin nodded. "I agree – most people. But it's amazing what you don't know about people. Seems like everybody's got a secret."

"Not me," she said. "I am an open book. I decided years ago it's just too complicated to pretend to be anything but what I am."

"I like that," Kevin said. And he meant it – he liked her air of genuine candor. Was anyone really that straightforward?

"No skeletons in your closet? Nothing you wish you hadn't done in your twenties? You never shoplifted a lipstick in high school? Or, like, threw out an ugly sweater from your grandmother and told your mom you lost it?" He was grinning at her.

She laughed. "OK, you win. But I don't count things that happened before I was fifteen. I did throw away my old roommate's magic mushrooms one time. I still feel bad about that."

"Oh, she must have been pissed!"

"It was an accident! I truly thought they were regular mushrooms, spoiled. What a dolt."

Glancing at the clock on the wall, Kevin suddenly remembered that he was going to be on call in a half hour. He started to tell her about it – apologizing in advance that if his beeper were to sound any time after eleven, he would have to rush to the scene for the big case he had mentioned, the one with the city cops. She gave him a look and asked, "For real? Or are you just trying to get rid of me?"

He smiled. "For real. Stay as long as you like."

"I think you're the one with the secrets," she teased.

He didn't want to go there. He could feel the wine making him melancholy, reminding him that his secrets were more sad than sexy. He thought of the secrets his father had carried, and the cost it had wreaked on his family. Of the secrets locked inside his mother's mind. His impulse was to deflect her attention away from himself.

"Take your friend, Deacon, for example." She frowned a little, puzzled.

"Did you know he works at the U?" He realized he had made a misstep; he wished he could unsay Deacon's name.

"Of course," she said.

"His name came up, purely by chance, when I was investigating financial transactions for that embezzlement case I told you about. I'm sure it's nothing."

"What are you saying?" Her puzzled expression shifted ever so slightly toward concern.

"Nothing – just that it's a small world, and like I said, it's amazing what you don't know about people."

"I know what I need to know. I know he's in recovery; he had some bad times but he's clean and sober. He's a loyal friend and one of the smartest people I know. There's no way he would steal from anyone, especially the college. He values his stability and sobriety more than anything." She raised her chin.

Still wishing his own words unsaid, Kevin said, "You're right, I'm sure. And I didn't mean to imply that he had done anything wrong. He's rough-looking but I'm sure he has a heart of gold."

"What's that supposed to mean?"

"You know, the tattoos...I mean, it's not surprising that the kind of people who hang out at an alternative place like the maker space would have colorful backgrounds."

"Have you been checking up on my friends?"

Again, Kevin tried to back off. "Like I said, his name came up on a financial report. I was just doing my job...I didn't even know he worked there. Funny that he didn't mention it when we met."

"Deacon is a pretty unusual name, and you remembered it." Sheila was still poking at the implications of Kevin's offhand comment; he didn't like being on the defensive.

"Right, and I thought it was a nickname – you called him _the_ Deacon," he answered, sounding weak even to himself.

"He's a good man. I've known him for years."

"Look, I'm sure you're right. Seems like everyone over at the maker space has some history. Artists, artisans, living on the fringe. Like I said, it's not surprising, for an alternative hangout like that."

Sheila sat bolt upright. "What do you mean, everyone?"

"Deacon, the two women..." He saw his mistake.

"I need to pee," Sheila said abruptly. She put down her glass, and got up, walking carefully back toward the bathroom in her bare legs and feet. Even at an angle, Kevin saw that her face was telling a whole new story – anger, fear, vulnerability. Kevin took a deep breath, alone now at the small table, cluttered with the chicken carcass and empty wine bottles. It felt very quiet. She was in the bathroom for a while. When she came out, she went directly into the bedroom and partially closed the door so she was out of sight. He could hear the sounds of clothing, and the whishing of legs being thrust quickly into jeans. The zipper.

"Are you OK? Sheila?" He got up and knocked,

suddenly feeling vulnerable himself in his shorts and bare feet.

"Excuse me," she said as she pulled the bedroom door open and found him blocking her way. Her face was pinched and blotchy with contained rage. Everything had turned. Kevin stepped aside.

"Sheila. I'm sorry; I didn't mean to upset you. I'm sure you are right about your friends. I shouldn't have mentioned it. That was wrong."

She passed by him and walked over to grab her purse off the table by the front door.

"What right do you have to investigate my friends? And then you invite me over here so that you can, what? Spring it on me? Watch me squirm? That's sick."

"Sheila…"

She held up a hand and Kevin was silent. With her other hand, she pulled the door open and stepped into the opening. Defiantly, she looked over her shoulder at him.

"We're done here. Don't call me." She sniffled, rubbing the back of her hand under her nose.

She left, slamming the door behind her.

Fuck, Kevin thought. Why couldn't I just shut the hell up? He looked back at the dirty plates, and then at the two pictures on the wall. Nothing had ever looked sadder or more disappointing. The lines were clumsy, almost clownish. Impulsively, he pulled them down and shoved them into the back of the closet, facing the wall. He pulled on his sweats. He didn't know what to do next. He dropped to the couch, his head in his hands, rocking with anger and frustration at his own idiocy. Hadn't he learned? Hadn't he told himself not to go there? He took a shower, fuming at himself as he let the hot water run over him and scrubbed his skin red. It was Heather all over again – why couldn't he ever just leave things alone? He wondered if he was unfixable, unfit for any real human relationship. He turned off the water and stood, head downcast, dripping as the cold air raised gooseflesh on his arms and legs.

Eventually, he grabbed a towel and dried off.

As he pulled his sweatpants back on, his mind turned toward action. Could he text an apology? She had said not to call. Maybe he should wait until tomorrow when she might have cooled off. He washed the dishes and finished the wine in a long gulp, raw and bitter in his throat. It had been thirty minutes since she left. He didn't know what to do next.

It was just past eleven p.m.; he was on duty now. He went to the bedroom and pulled the beeper out of his jeans, dropping it on the coffee table as he fell back defeated onto the couch. He thought about going to see Deacon to enlist his support, but then knew that was a terrible idea. Maybe Jason would put in a good word for him. He snorted at the humiliation of asking for the kid's help. One part of his mind was sure it was over but another part couldn't let go. He reached for the remote to turn on SportsCenter, looking for some distraction from his racing, circling thoughts.

Chapter 20 – Classic Forensic Accounting

For the rest of the weekend, Kevin was tortured by the silence of two devices: the motion sensor buzzer, as usual, and now his own cellphone. He was embarrassed by how frequently he checked it, hoping that Sheila might call. The resounding silence in his condo left plenty of space for Kevin to berate himself for botching things with Sheila. He didn't know where he'd gotten such a special talent for self-sabotage. Why did he keep lobbing grenades in the path toward companionship? All day Sunday, he mentally composed apologetic notes to her, even as he resisted the urge to send them.

Returning to work on Monday morning was a relief because he could stay busy doing all the usual stuff – following up on the petty details of other cases, tracking down the data from the phone records, surfing the web, making coffee, and then drinking it. Even getting called in for traffic duty was a welcome distraction from his own thoughts. He grabbed a late sandwich with Rafiq, who asked, "Whatever happened with that woman you were dating?" Kevin couldn't bear to go into it, so he just said, "Yeah, I don't think that's gonna work out."

Late Monday afternoon, he was once again standing outside a conference room, this time in the student travel office, while Larry, HR, and a hapless middle manager took down another petty thief. P-cards again. The door opened.

It was the same drill - no extra excitement in it this time. When the perp came out of the room, Kevin saw that she was a hunched-over woman in late middle-age. She had a wet ball of Kleenex in her right hand and she kept jamming the back of her wrist against her glasses, pushing them further up the bridge of her nose while apologizing.

"I knew I shouldn't do it, but my daughter thought it would be okay," she said. "She needed things for the baby; she said her boyfriend does it all the time at his job," she said.

"I'll walk you to your desk," Kevin said.

"The university is so rich. I didn't think anyone would notice," she said.

Kevin wanted to shush her. She was incriminating herself, not that it mattered much. But he stayed silent; his job was to stand by while she gathered her personal effects, then escort her out of the building.

"I started to take it for granted. It was so easy, like maybe it was really okay. But I knew it wasn't," she said. Kevin almost felt sorry for her.

When they got to her area, she looked even more epically pathetic. She meekly asked him to wait outside. "Look through the glass, you can watch me the whole time. Please don't escort me in; it's too humiliating." She nodded toward the other workers, heads down at their cubes. "They look up to me," she said. Kevin doubted it, but he nodded. It seemed like a kindness.

When it was all over, he walked her out, then headed back to Larry's building to debrief.

Larry was characteristically cheerful. "We only have a few more on the termination list. We are making great progress! Man, that lady didn't even seem to do anything worthwhile with her money." Kevin looked over his shoulder.

"What do you mean?"

"Classic forensic accounting, baby. A simple

google property search can turn up some very interesting data. But not this time. She lives in a crap apartment three towns away. Hard to tell what she was spending all that money on."

Kevin was tempted to say *diapers,* but he let it go. "Check her emergency contact." He went to get a cup of coffee – the internal audit group had a high-end pod machine that was way better than the swill over at CAMPO. Larry tapped away at his keyboard. By the time Kevin returned, Larry was even more cheerful. "Bingo. Good call." Her daughter had a brand-new house in a tony suburb. Google Streetview showed a late-model Lexus in the driveway.

"Huh," Kevin said, leaning toward the screen. "Do the same search on Dory Johnson."

"You seem obsessed with her. She your latest Tinder flame?" asked Larry. Kevin barked out a short laugh.

"Love that public information. Let's see…She's got two properties listed. One is a little ranch, a few blocks from campus, nothing exciting. And here's the second one…."

They both caught their breath; Larry let out a slow whistle. "Holy baloney."

They were looking at an aerial shot – the kind used in high end real estate ads. It was a waterfront property in Greyport, on a small peninsula jutting out into the ocean. The house was shingle-style and modest. Sparkling white Adirondack chairs were scattered on the perfect lawn. But what drew their attention was the boat. It was moored against a well-built dock, in front of a small boathouse. Kevin wasn't sure what to call it, maybe a small yacht? But it was a beauty, gleaming white with polished wood decks on three levels, and shining hardware.

"That must be deep water right there, to allow a cruiser like that to pull up," Larry said.

"The waterfront lot, the boat…it sure doesn't

square with working as a building super," Kevin observed.

Larry nodded at the screen, "That is some serious bank." Then he turned to face Kevin, "Wait, is this the lady with the missing receipt authorizations?" Kevin nodded, and Larry whistled again, low and slow. Kevin said, "Email me that link," thinking he needed to get back to headquarters ASAP and show it to Mulally.

Chapter 21 – The Buzzer At Last

On Tuesday, Kevin was back in Figure Drawing. It was the last class of the term, but Kevin wasn't feeling the usual "end of the semester" sense of accomplishment and closure.

Jason bounded over, seeming even younger than usual in his happy enthusiasm.

"Hey man, thanks again for hooking me up with Artemis. You won't believe it – she gave me an internship in the etching department. I'm gonna make fifteen bucks an hour cataloging their collection, starting right after exams. This is sweet. I owe you, man!" He held up his right hand for a high-five.

Kevin reached up and met Jason's palm, smiling. "That's terrific! You deserve it. I'm happy for you."

He hoped his low spirits didn't show. Being in drawing class had triggered his mind to restart running loops of the disastrous date with Sheila. Tonight, he was wondering if his work had twisted him into someone who always looked for the worst in people. No surprise, these thoughts made it hard to concentrate, even though the model was a skilled poser, reasonably young and fit like Greek statuary. But for Kevin, the joy had gone out of it. The charcoal felt clumsy and dry in his hand.

And then the buzzer in his pocket went off. His

first impulse was to slap it into silence through his pantleg; as he did so, his heart started beating double time and every hair on his head shot to life. His stomach turned over.

He grabbed his backpack and bolted, knocking over the chair as he rushed to the door. He called for city cop backup as he hustled across campus on foot. He arrived at Waverly in just a few minutes, confirmed that there was a light in the apartment, and then stood in the shadows to wait. Reaching into his pack, he put on his service belt then dropped the bag in the bushes, trying to steady his breathing. Within another minute, Smitty rounded the corner in full uniform. Noting Smitty's girth for the first time, Kevin hoped they wouldn't have to give chase. Smitty unclipped his gun before they entered the building and walked slowly down the empty hall together. Kevin rapped on the door to 12C with the back of his hand as he said loudly, "University Police, open up."

He hoped Smitty couldn't hear his heart thumping.

"We're coming in," he shouted, and he put the key in the lock.

Crashing sounds came from within, and they felt the floor shift as someone headed toward the door. Both cops braced themselves, each with his right hand on his belt. The door flew open, revealing an enormous naked woman with her hands up. "Don't shoot! don't shoot! I'm innocent," she shouted, lowering her arms to cover her massive breasts, her ten fingers looking tiny against all that flesh. She must have been six foot two and two-eighty, tits flanked by a puffy neck, three rolls of padding around her middle, and two colossal thighs. She looked like a bottle blond lady Michelin Man.

Kevin saw it all in a split second, then heard a noise in the back of the apartment. "Step aside, ma'am," and he pushed past her into the room. When he got to the bedroom, the window was open and there was no one there. Goddamn first floor apartment. He scanned the grounds outside, seeing nothing in the darkening twilight. He checked the closet and the bathroom, both empty. When he leaned down to check under the bed, the smell of shit hit his nostrils and he saw the smear on the sheets – not five inches from his face. He thought he might puke.

There was a hundred-dollar bill on the bedside table. Kevin picked up a coat from the chair and brought it back to where Smitty was still holding his gun up in both hands, keeping the woman cowering in fear. "Here, put this on. Cover yourself up." As she slowly reached for the coat, her hands in surrender mode, he saw her golden fingernails and the fact that she wasn't fully naked: high-heeled sandals were wrapped tightly around her puffy feet.

"You're gonna need to come back to the station with us, ma'am." His police training kicked in; he instinctively used the artificially deferential language that seemed to calm down perps and suspects.

"I'll tell you everything I know," she wailed. "I don't want any trouble." As soon as her coat was fastened, Smitty reached over and put handcuffs on her.

She whimpered, "Is that really necessary? I'm not resisting arrest."

"Procedure, lady," Smitty said. Kevin doubted it, but he knew better than to break ranks at a crucial moment. His heart was still pumping against his shirt.

"Let's go," Smitty said, leading her into the hallway.

When the three of them stepped outside the building together, the scene was surreal. Smitty's partner had pulled the patrol car up to the front of the building, right on the sidewalk, and had kept his blue lights spinning. The garish, rotating lights cast a scary haze over the courtyard, usually so peaceful. Students who happened to be nearby stood gawking from the perimeter, their ghostly presence signaled by the flashes on their phones, as they silently shot video of the police action.

Hamish was there, standing by the cruiser with Smitty's partner. Intermittent rasps and alerts from the police radio, turned up loud, pierced the quiet. They put the woman into the back seat, then stood there quietly sharing information about what they had seen in the room.

"I'll need to do a quick walk-through," Hamish said.

Kevin nodded. "You guys go ahead; I'll brief Mulally. Any chance we can turn off the flashers in the meantime?"

"Good idea. Smitty, come with me. Pina, move the cruiser into that lot over there, and kill the disco lights. Conley, hang tight. You should come downtown with us. Be there for the questioning of the suspect."

Hamish nodded to the other officer, "Keep an eye on her."

Officer Pina reached into the cab and switched off the lights. As he did so, he called out, "OK, everybody. The show's over. Everything is OK – keep walking." Kevin stepped into a shadow, away from the onlookers, and dialed Mulally.

Chapter 22 – A Runner

Around eleven o'clock that night, Kevin wearily pushed open the door to his silent condo and dropped his keys on the counter, the first sound to echo through the room in hours. Throughout the drive home, his mind played over and over the scene at City headquarters. As he reached for the refrigerator door, his phone pinged with an emergency alert. It was from Mulally, directed to the whole CAMPO force.

9:00 AM FULL BRIEFING WAVERLY HALL INCIDENT. CONLEY TO LEAD. DON'T BE LATE.

Jesus, he thought. Thanks for the heads-up. He reached into the fridge for a beer, then took a moment to ponder whether drinking it would help him make sense of the jumbled information on his notepad. He decided it would. In fact, he nodded to himself, it would be essential. He reached for the bottle opener, jimmied the lid for that satisfying pop of a bending bottle cap, and reached for his laptop. While it hummed to life, he took a long swig and let out a loud, *Ahh…* OK, he thought. We'll take this chronologically to capture every key event and piece of evidence as they were revealed. He pulled his pad from his back pocket, slapped it on the counter in front of him, and started typing.

In the morning, he still felt keyed up. He shaved

and dressed with more care than usual, even giving his shoes a quick buff. Walking into the office fifteen minutes early, he was only a little surprised to see, through the conference room window, Hamish and Smitty huddled with Mulally, their heads bowed together in intense conversation. Everyone else on the force was present, trying to look busy at their desks. Rafiq brought him a cup of coffee, "You ready, man?" Kevin nodded and walked toward the conference room door, his laptop under his arm.

At exactly nine, Mulally opened the conference room door and invited the rest of the team in. All eight of them squeezed into the room. With Hamish and Smitty there, two of the newer guys had to stand against the back wall. Kevin snapped his laptop open as the group settled in.

Mulally reminded everyone about the case, gesturing toward "our colleagues from the city," and saying in a droll tone, "I'm sure you heard about the excitement over on West Campus last night. Kevin Conley, who has been lead detective on this investigation, will walk us through the events."

Kevin picked up the thread from the time the beeper sounded, at about 7:15 p.m. when he was in a classroom building on the main quad. There were only a few snickers when he described the scene in apartment 12C, quickly silenced by a scowl from Mulally. Up to this point in the story, much of the information Kevin was sharing had already been circulating among the CAMPO force, in more or less outlandish versions. It was when the scene moved downtown that the story fell on fresh ears. Kevin continued more slowly now.

"At approximately 8:10, we departed the campus and headed downtown. Officer Smith and his partner transported the suspect in the cruiser. I traveled with Detective Hamish. We arrived at police headquarters at 8:25. Officer Smith booked the suspect. She contacted a friend to post bail. Both the suspect and the friend were subsequently questioned in relation to the murder investigation. Officer Smith, Detective Hamish, and I were all in the room during questioning.

"We questioned the suspect at 9:00 pm. She was calm and cooperative. According to police records, this was her third time being brought in on prostitution charges. The suspect stated that she was a sex worker and has utilized the Waverly Hall apartment roughly ten times before, starting one year ago. She was given a key to the unit by her agent, aka her pimp, and had it in her possession. We confiscated the key. She stated that her agent would text her appointments and locations. The Waverly apartment was one of several locations around the city. Officer Smith confiscated additional keys for other locations.

"The suspect stated that she was acquainted with the murder victim, Tiffany Matthews. She described Tiffany as a 'new girl' who didn't know the ropes. She believed Tiffany was using drugs and not behaving in a professional manner." Here Kevin used air quotes to indicate that this was a direct quote. "She believed that Tiffany may have been freelancing, to avoid splitting her fee. She believed this because Ms. Matthews had complained more than once about getting ripped off by the agent; the agent had also referred to Matthews as a junkie on one occasion."

Kevin turned toward the city guys. "Any further clarifications or updates regarding the suspect?" They shook their heads and Kevin continued.

"The friend who came in to post bail for the suspect admitted, under questioning, that he was an agent for sex workers. He was given the keys by someone who told him they came from the building super, who offered the use of the premises as collateral for an extension on outstanding gambling debts. He claimed to know nothing more; he could not recall who gave him the keys. He stated that he had given copies of the keys to a few of the sex workers. He appeared to be under the influence and was held in the station overnight to dry out.

"The agent posted bail for the suspect. She was cleared to leave on her own recognizance. Do you have anything to add, Detectives Hamish and Smith?"

"No, thanks for the excellent summary. We'll question the pimp as soon as we're done here," said Hamish.

Mulally slapped his big hands on the table. "OK, thank you Detective Conley. Folks, we'll keep the motion sensor active in case there are other keys floating among the outside element, so stick with the current rotation. Obviously, we will have Buildings & Grounds change the locks today. During your regular rounds, please pay special attention to the area around Waverly. Keep a calm but frequent presence in the area to reassure people."

He turned to address Kevin directly. "Turns out the super called in sick today." There was a buzz through the room. "Try to raise her on her emergency number. I've set up an urgent meeting with the general counsel at one o'clock; you'll need to be there."

Mulally turned back to the group. "And I don't need to remind you, but no one talks to the press, especially the student press. Any information that leaks out in the next few days could jeopardize the murder investigation. Conley is on point; any new information or leads go direct to him. Let's get to work."

Everyone rose from their chairs. As Rafiq passed Kevin, he clasped his shoulder. "Nice work," he murmured. Kevin nodded.

Kevin went back to his desk long enough to get Dory Johnson's personal cell number through the HR system. He brought the digits back into the conference room and dialed her on the speakerphone, with Hamish, Smith, and Mulally still in the room. She picked up on the fourth ring.

"Dory," he said. "This is Kevin Conley from CAMPO. I hear you're off campus today?"

"Yeah," she said in that unmistakable raspy voice. "And I hear there was excitement in my building last night. Another break-in?"

"Something like that," Kevin replied. "The chief and I want to bring you up-to-speed. Can you come in today?"

"I'm out on a family matter," she said. "I'll call you when I'm back. I heard the city cops were there last night. What gives?" Kevin and Mulally locked eyes and shook their heads silently to each other.

"We'll talk about it when you come in. Come to CAMPO headquarters first thing tomorrow."

"Look, I've worked at this place for fifteen years; I've got more accumulated sick and vacation time than Jesus himself. I'll come in when my family matter allows." She hung up. Kevin double-clicked the desk phone, then lifted and dropped the receiver on its cradle, to make sure the connection was broken. He looked up at the others.

"Ballsy!" said Hamish. "A family matter? I think we've got a runner here. We staked out her house last night; no evidence that anyone was there."

"Tell them about the Greyport property," Mulally instructed.

Kevin turned back to his laptop and pulled up the real estate listing on his laptop. "She has another place, in Greyport. I've got the address. And guys – she has a boat." He spun the laptop around so they could see the image.

As they leaned in, Smitty said, "Nice. And this lady's a building super? What, is she married to Warren Buffett?"

Hamish pulled out his phone, saying, "I know a guy down there." Within seconds, he had a local Greyport cop driving toward the property. They refilled their coffee cups as they waited for the phone to ring back. When his phone rang, Hamish answered, "Thanks, man. I'm putting you on speaker." And set his phone on the conference table.

A tinny voice responded. "I'm here at the property now. Nice place! No sign of any disturbance. Car in the driveway, a late model Bronco. The license plate is registered to one Doreen Johnson. I can see the dock from here; it's empty. No boat. You want me to call the harbormaster?"

"Yeah," said Hamish. "Text me back what he says."

Hamish and Smitty prepared to return downtown. Hamish insisted that he would return to campus for the general counsel meeting that afternoon.

"It'll be harder for them to act like pussies if I'm there," he said. Mulally and Kevin let it go; they might have expressed it differently, but they didn't disagree.

"In the meantime," said Hamish, "we'll interrogate the pimp, who has hopefully slept off whatever made him so unforthcoming last night."

Smitty chuckled at his boss's choice of words. "Fancy! I think this place is rubbing off on you."

As the four men walked toward the exit together, they head the familiar ping of a text arriving. Hamish squinted at his phone.

"She took the boat out last night; has not yet returned." He looked up at the other three men. "Gentlemen, we've got a runner."

The General Counsel's office was in Harker Hall, the same building where the President sat, and all too recently for Kevin, the building where Carmelo Jones had been taken down. He was starting to feel like a regular. It was even the same conference room, except last time Kevin had stood outside the closed door. Today, a polished young woman ushered Kevin, Hamish and Mulally into the room and cooed at them to wait.

"Sandra Chu, general counsel, and Marilyn Burns, head of HR, will be in shortly." She pulled the door shut behind her with a heavy click.

Hamish observed, "Sounds like when you shut the door on a C-series Benz."

"Like we would know," countered Mulally, but his voice was hushed. Hamish walked the perimeter of the room, tracing his fingers along the walls and inspecting the recessed lights over each painting.

It was a far cry from the setup at CAMPO. The room was paneled and painted a creamy, lustrous ivory. Anyone invited in would be soothed by the millwork camouflaging whatever technology and screens might be there. Framed drawings, leather-bound books, and well-lit antiquities, probably selected by Artemis Johns herself, were scattered about. Thick carpeting muted the soundscape, presumably eliminating the possibility of discord or miscommunication. As Kevin looked around, he wondered if the magic would work today.

The two women came in together and shook hands all around. Kevin had never met Sandra Chu before. She was petite and severely dressed, her hair cut blunt at chin length. She was also visibly annoyed and voluble, telling them immediately, "I spent last night and most of the morning dealing with the press. Everyone wants to know what's going on here; why the city cops were on campus. I'd like to hear more about that myself."

Mulally briefed them on the case, reminding Chu that her office had approved the motion sensors and that he had informed them of the cooperation with the city. With remarkably few well-chosen words, he brought them up to date – including Dory's embezzlement and the fact that, having heard about the arrest the night before, she had not come to work that day.

"Given the combination of factors here," said Mulally, "our next step is to bring in Dory Johnson. We recommend that the university press felony charges against her for grand theft."

Chu frowned at him over her half-rims. "We have no evidence that she's implicated in the murder. All we have is the simple misuse of funds – and as Detective Conley knows, we have a procedure in place for handling that. I don't see the need to escalate."

Hamish turned a darker shade of red. "Johnson is, at the very least, a material witness in a murder. We have strong reason to believe she is AWOL – a fugitive – which doesn't exactly suggest innocence. She needs a strong incentive to testify so we can solve this thing. I don't give a fuck about the newspapers. She is in the direct line to getting justice for Tiffany Matthews."

Chu rolled her eyes. "Jesus, Hamish. You're such a drama queen." Hamish smiled and cocked his head. For a split-second Kevin wondered, was he flirting? With the general counsel?

Kevin gathered his wits. "Based on the evidence, the magnitude on the embezzlement is well above simple theft; she has committed a felony. Given the lifestyle we can observe through public sources, this has probably been going on for years. She appears to have a gambling problem, which exacerbates the risk – both for her and for the university."

Marilyn Burns broke in, "Oh, there's no question of her coming back to work, you know that, Kevin."

Mulally spread his hands and leaned forward. "Folks, this individual risked community safety by allowing – really *inviting* - a criminal element onto our campus." Here he stabbed the mahogany table with a firm finger. "This isn't about the money. I think we all know that. For justice to be served, and for the safety of our students, we need to bring the full force of the law to this case."

There was a pause. All five of them looked around, one to the next, knowing that the community safety argument was *checkmate*.

The attorney leaned back and said, "Christ, you guys. I mean, did you really need to put cuffs on the lady last night? Did you need to pull the cruiser right up onto the quad, and leave the red and blues flashing for almost an hour? You scared people half to death."

Kevin could see the victory in Hamish's eyes, but he kept his face straight.

"We'll terminate Dory Johnson based on malfeasance. I'll have the paperwork ready for when she's brought in," said Marilyn.

"OK," agreed Chu. "And yeah, this rises to the level where we press charges against Johnson. But can we try to proceed with less operatic flair from here on out? I mean, Hamish, you know the university wants to cooperate with you guys, but c'mon. How about a little finesse."

He smiled, holding her gaze. "I'll see what we can do."

Hamish, Kevin, and Mulally walked back across the quad, enjoying the little victory. It was just before two, and the sun was trying to pierce the slate gray sky. A few yards away, six stalwart students ran in circles with broomsticks between their legs, tossing a ball around.

Hamish glanced in their direction and said, "I won't ask."

Kevin answered anyway, "Believe it or not, it's some Harry Potter thing."

A tour group strolled by, led by a young guy with big hair and glasses, walking backward as he described the function of the blue emergency light pillars. Despite the chill in the air, the families looked eager and proud, imagining their kids thriving in this city of learning. Kevin tried to stay focused on what Hamish was saying.

"Now it's simple. Kevin, you call her up again and lay it on the line. Scare the shit out of her. Tell her we know about the grifting, the gambling, the pimps and the prostitutes. Tell her we're investigating a murder and with all this evidence, she's a suspect. Tell her we're sending the Coast Guard to drag her sorry ass back to shore. She'll buy it. As she showed this morning, she thinks you're too dumb to be a bullshitter. She'll think you're helping her out."

Mulally nodded. "Sounds like a plan. Hamish, one of your guys can call the Coast Guard; your buddy in Greyport can get the identifying features and registration on her boat." They nodded good-byes and split off, with Mulally and Kevin heading back to CAMPO. As they walked through the main door, one of the new guys handed Mulally a pink phone message memo.

"Jesus, what next?" asked Mulally as he gestured to Kevin. "Follow me. It's from Fensbridge."

In his office, Mulally punched in the numbers using the speakerphone, and for once, Fensbridge answered on the first ring.

"Chief Mulally," he said, suddenly a beacon of respect. "I got a call just now from Dory Johnson and wanted to let you know. She's worried about her job; worried that she's made a few, ah, mistakes and asked for my help. She mentioned that she is out on her boat and thinking of, ah, not coming back.

"OK," said Mulally. "Anything else?"

"She tried to blackmail me about the apartment. I told her you already know all about it, so she should save her breath. I stopped her before she could say much. No need for me to be implicated in this tawdry matter. I told her there had been a murder, and she should come in and clear her name. I told her there's nothing I could do. I don't think she's connected to the murder, but, well, who knows what goes on in people's heads. I just thought you should know."

Mulally thanked him, told him to call again if she reached out, and pressed the release button. He looked up at Kevin. "I guess we're besties now."

Kevin was too annoyed to acknowledge the sarcasm. "He told her about the murder. That was idiotic."

Mulally shrugged. "Agreed, but it probably won't make much difference. Did he actually say *tawdry?* Who talks like that?"

Kevin shook his head. "I love the fact that <u>now</u> he's worried about being implicated…"

"What a piece of work. You hungry? We skipped lunch. Let's get a burger. We can call Johnson when we get back."

"I love how you're so calm in the middle of all this, Chief," Kevin said, with real admiration in his voice.

"Don't call me Chief," said Mulally, smiling.

So again, just like on the day they had ordered the motion detector, the wheels were in motion. The Coast Guard was tracking Dory's vessel and would bring her in. It might take a day or two. All they could do was wait. Hamish would keep working his angles downtown to find the killer. Hopefully, Waverly 12C would stay quiet now that the locks were being changed. The daily routines of CAMPO would rise to fill the time.

Chapter 23 - Dory Spills

On Thursday, Kevin's most fervent wish for a quiet day was granted. He spent the morning catching up on paperwork, making sure that all the reports were filed on the Waverly 12C investigation and wrapping up the P-cards work. He chatted with Larry Melnick – he couldn't share any details but wanted Larry to know that the real estate info had proven essential to one of his cases. When Larry asked if it had anything to do with the big brouhaha on West Campus, Kevin just chuckled knowingly, enjoying his moment as the one with the inside scoop.

"Who's the muscle now, amirite?" Larry asked. They agreed to grab a beer next week, to celebrate their progress catching the worst of the P-card offenders.

Next, Kevin closed the loop with Mary Sue Flanagan over in the chemistry department. Fortunately, things there had checked out okay; it didn't look like the Jack the Masturbator situation was going to haunt anything but Kevin's visual memory. That was a relief. The rest of the day was mundane: he went to Starbucks for dark roast, ran a few errands, and ate a grilled chicken wrap at Brad's Place with Rafiq.

Mid-afternoon, he had a sudden idea and shot off

a quick email to Marilyn Burns over in Human Resources.

> *Marilyn,*
> *When that position for a new super at Waverly opens up, take a look at Reinaldo Reyes – cleaning crew chief. He's a good guy – smart and motivated. You can call me if you need a character witness. – Kevin*

Almost immediately, he got a reply:

> *His ears must be burning. I just got a "thumbs up" on him from Lloyd Deacon over at Masterman. Two unimpeachable sources – thanks! - M*

Her unexpected mention of Deacon cracked open a dull pain in Kevin's gut. He took a deep breath, regretting anew his bungling with Sheila. Reflecting that this had been a good week, he called on his faith in lucky streaks and reached for his phone. His thumbs spelled out *I'm sorry. I was an idiot. I hope you'll call me.* He looked at the message for a few seconds, wondering if he had hit the right note of humble conciliation. Then he shrugged and pressed send. He watched his phone for a few seconds, but there were no rhythmic *dot dot dots.* Kevin sighed, aware that it was probably the end of that road.

Early Friday morning, Kevin was just getting into his car to drive to work when his phone buzzed with a text from Rafiq. *Dory Johnson just walked in. I put her in conference room. Mulally on his way.* Kevin texted back: *I'll be there in twenty. Don't let her leave.* Then he texted the same information to Hamish. Nerves jangling, he screeched his tires making the sharp turn out of the driveway.

Kevin and Hamish arrived together at the front door of CAMPO headquarters. Kevin held the door, trying to cover his nerves with this gesture of camaraderie. As Hamish passed through, Kevin felt the connection between them had become real. They had come a long way together; they understood how each other thought and worked. Hamish was no longer the Big Cop from the city and Kevin was no longer the kid. They had done good work together and were nearing the resolution. It was a good feeling.

"So she wasn't much of a runner after all, I guess," Kevin said.

"You gownies are all too soft for life on the lam," Hamish replied. Kevin shook his head. Maybe the deep connection he felt in that moment was one-sided after all.

"That's a new one. *Gownies*? Is that what the cool kids are saying now?"

As they walked inside, they saw Mulally already at his desk and Dory seated alone in the conference room, her back to the window. Kevin noted she was still wearing her gold university polo and hoodie – she was dressed for work. Rafiq sat outside the conference room door, guarding it. Kevin nodded to him, then he and Hamish went straight into Mulally's office.

"OK," Mulally said when they had shut the door, his eyes trained on Hamish. "Here's how this is going to go. She is in our jurisdiction, she is still an employee with rights, and I am going to take the lead on this interrogation. Hamish, no BS this time. You can get aggressive with the university lawyers, but not with the union employees. You got any follow-up questions, you ask me and I'll ask her. You got it?" Hamish nodded. "HR will meet her here after we finish the questioning."

"We'll try it your way. As soon as she's terminated, she's mine anyway," Hamish grumbled.

Mulally cleared his throat and rose heavily, signaling that their briefing was complete. They walked together to the conference room. As they filed past Rafiq, Mulally said to him, "Great work. Much appreciated." Kevin entered last, nodding at Rafiq, and closed the door behind him.

"Thanks for coming in, Dory," said Mulally,

dropping a legal pad and pencil on the table. He introduced the others. "Can we get you a cup of coffee? Water?" She shook her head. The three men sat down, one person on each side of the table.

Mulally continued. "OK. I'm gonna be straight with you. It's a messy situation. I'll tell you what we know and then we need to ask you a few questions. You have the right to remain silent…"

"Am I under arrest?" she interrupted, incredulous.

"There are serious allegations here; you need to understand your rights before questioning." Mulally continued reciting the Miranda rights. Dory sat back, crossing her arms over her chest.

"We have strong evidence that you have been systematically embezzling funds from the university. This alone is sufficient for your arrest for felony, grand larceny. You have also been accused of giving access – keys – to university property to criminals, specifically a prostitution ring. A girl was murdered recently in town. Tiffany Matthews, a prostitute. The cops found a two a.m. appointment in Waverly Hall in her cell phone."

"I don't know anything about any murder. I've worked here for fifteen years – you're gonna try to pin me with some junkie hooker's murder?"

Kevin broke in, "Who said anything about a junkie?"

Dory was silent.

"Dory, there is the matter of the stolen funds. The evidence of criminal wrongdoing is very clear. You're probably going to jail on that one alone." Mulally looked almost sad to be laying out these facts; Kevin was struck by the kindness on Mulally's drooping face. "How you answer our questions might make a difference in how this all turns out. I gotta say, your boat excursion made us wonder if you were going to come back at all."

She looked down at her hands.

"I got scared. That was a mistake. I saw Hamish at

Waverly that night, and I got worried. Everybody knows
he's a murder cop."

Kevin blurted, "You were there that night? Why
didn't you check in with me?"

"Like I said, I got scared. The situation was way
out of hand."

Mulally nodded. "It's good that you came back. So
what was going on?"

Dory sighed, blinking back tears. She raised both
hands to her head and grabbed fistfuls of her hair. From
this awkward stance, she started to talk, looking down at
the table in front of her. "I owed some money and I
couldn't pay it back fast enough. The apartment was, like,
collateral they were using while I got the cash together. It
got out of control. I told them it was too hot, but they
thought I was welching on the debt."

Mulally continued to nod. She dropped her hands
back into her lap and seemed to recover some of her
bravado. She looked back at him and shrugged.

"How much money did you take from the
university?" Mulally asked.

"Hardly any – I don't know about your 'evidence,'
but it's peanuts. You can't make it stick," she said with
disdain. "I make my real money playing poker. I'm the
nuts. A real monster."

Mulally's face stayed quiet and sad. "I don't know
what you mean by 'hardly any.' In this state, grand larceny
is anything over a thousand dollars, and the forensic
accounting indicates you've taken five times that just in the
past couple years. You put this community in danger.
That's not nothing. The university is gonna press charges,
and you face prison time. If you have information toward
solving this murder, you need to share it. It could make a
difference in your sentencing." The room was silent.

"What about the victim? Tiffany?" Mulally
pressed.

"I've never heard of her. I never met anyone;

none of that lot. I gave one key to my bookie. That's it. I didn't like the looks of some of those people, so I never talked to any of them. Just cleaned up their messes." She grimaced in disgust at the memories and sank lower into the hard chair.

Mulally sighed and leaned back. "OK, we're going to take a little break. You stay here. If you think of anything, write it down." He pushed the yellow pad and pencil across the table toward her. "Can we bring you anything?"

Slumped there, Dory Johnson shook her head. As they stood to leave, Kevin had to ask a question that had plagued him since the beginning.

"Dory, why'd you call in that stolen etching in the first place? That's been bugging me."

She looked up, doleful.

"I thought you guys being around might scare them off, that's all. I didn't expect it to snowball like this. I just wanted a little time and space to work it out. I've almost got the money now. Everything back to normal."

Normal, thought Kevin doubtfully. Not likely. Looking up, he saw through the glass behind her that Marilyn Burns had arrived. It was time for the next step: Dory would be terminated, relieved of her ID and keychain. Her electronic access – email and the like – were probably already gone.

Mulally stood up. "Marilyn Burns is here to talk with you now. Dory, I wish you well." The three men left the room together and closed the door behind them. Dory remained slumped in the chair, not turning around to see what was in store.

Mulally huddled with Marilyn, Hamish, and Kevin in the open area. "I think we got what we needed, and she admitted to the embezzlement. She's all yours, Marilyn. Once the termination is complete, Kevin will walk her over to Waverly to pick up her personal effects, then release her into Hamish's custody."

Marilyn cut in, "What's her state of mind?"

"Calm and about as docile as she's capable of. No undue concerns – the termination should go smoothly," Mulally responded.

"I'd like Detective Conley to join me when I speak to her now," she said. Mulally glanced at Kevin, who nodded.

"I'll drive over to the building in the cruiser and meet you there," said Hamish.

Marilyn and Mulally spoke together, "Keep a low profile. No flashers." They all smiled grimly, remembering the general counsel's warning.

"I get it," Mulally snickered. "I'll stay in the car and try to look like I'm having a donut; just blending in with the peaceful surroundings."

Kevin said, "You can wait in the back of that parking lot – I'll bring her over." Logistics established, they each proceeded with their part of the plan.

Chapter 24 - Debriefing

A couple of weeks later, just after the Thanksgiving break, Hamish called Mulally to let CAMPO know they had solved the murder of Tiffany Matthews. He wanted to close the loop, and suggested they debrief over a beer.

They met at six o'clock on a Wednesday night at a distressed-looking townie bar halfway between the university and the main precinct. It was the four men who were closest to the case: Kevin, Hamish, Mulally, and Smitty, all dressed in civvies. The place had an enclosed concrete patio out back with a couple of space heaters so that customers could smoke a cigarette with their beer, like in the old days. Mulally offered to get the first round, including "one of those fancy beers you like…" for Kevin, but Kevin knew Mulally drank Bud Light, so that's what he asked for, looking longingly at the microbrew taps on the bar. Mulally got him a local IPA anyway. "You like what you like," he said with a smirk.

Smitty was still playing catch-up on some of the early-stage campus details. "Let me get this straight. So, the building manager in one of your fancy dorms was on the take, trying to cover a little gambling problem. And her bookie put the screws to her for some old debts, and the deal was she had to let him use vacant apartments for his side business running prostitutes. So she gives him the keys but tries to keep an eye on things just in case?"

"Right," said Hamish. "Tiffany was one of the prostitutes, which was why the address showed up in her calendar. According to the big lady with the nails that you guys busted that night. "

"I call her Goldfinger," broke in Kevin.

"Nice," Hamish chuckled. "A good handle makes it easier to keep the villains straight. Anyway, according to Goldfinger, Tiffany was a problem from the start. She was sometimes high; not a professional. Didn't know how to handle herself."

Smitty snorted, rolling his eyes at the idea of hookers being professional.

"Hey," said Hamish, "Every profession's got its code. Building blocks of human society. I don't see anyone offering to pay you cash money for some action. You might see the world different if somebody offered."

"You got that right," Smitty looked dejectedly into his beer, silenced by being called out in front of the others.

"Anyway, she was off duty the night she was killed, and our theory was that she was freelancing. Nobody was keeping an eye on her; nobody was checking in at the end of a trick. She broke the code."

Mulally said dejectedly, "She was a kid. She probably wasn't even hooking long enough to appreciate those check-ins were keeping her alive." He shook his head. "It's a damn shame."

"How did you crack the case?" asked Kevin.

"We cut a deal with the bookie-slash-pimp. He gave us the names of the johns that had asked for Tiffany. There were nine guys. We cross-checked their records for drug priors: four guys. Compared the details of their drug priors to the drugs we found in her system: two guys. Went to interview the two guys who fit the profile best. One of them cracked right open when we said her name."

Smitty piped in, "I mean, he tried to deny it, but he was sweating, eyes shifting all over the room, he was a wreck. As soon as we mentioned the DNA match, he asked for a lawyer."

"You had DNA on the guy?" Mulally looked interested.

"Well, I sort of suggested that we had his DNA on file from his prior," said Hamish with a brief sly grin, obviously relishing the story.

"Which wasn't exactly true," added Smitty.

"But it did the trick. He didn't exactly confess, he just started saying she was a sweet girl, they liked hanging out, they were just having a good time…"

"Yeah, like the whole thing was some kind of 'rough sex' accident." Smitty interrupted again, but a sideways glare from Hamish shut him down mid-sentence.

Hamish continued. "But being thrown around wasn't her thing. We knew that from the bookie, from Goldfinger, from her friend at the dog pound. He was just a malicious prick. The way I see it, he roofied her, choked and raped her, and left her like garbage when she didn't come to. The fact that he dumped her like that instead of trying to get some help when she OD'd – we can all agree that undermined his story."

"Ultimately, he got his lawyer and we got his DNA. It checked out 100%. He's in jail now awaiting trial. He's going down." Hamish looked around the patio, with its splintery picnic tables and ashy potted plants, satisfied with this end to the story. "Truth is, that girl was taking a lot of chances with her life."

Mulally asked, "Are you suggesting she deserved it?" His voice was calm but his gaze was direct.

"I never said that. I'm just saying she was swimming with a lot of sharks." His voice had already written her off, ready to move on to the next case.

Each man took a pull from his beer. Kevin was thinking about Tiffany, who wanted to be a stand-up comic and liked dogs, but who had lost faith in her future enough to start mixing with lowlifes and heroin. He thought about the students on campus, and all the people who worked there, smoothing the path toward a bright future for those kids. Wasn't there a way to expand that altruism to include someone like Tiffany? There was a lull in the conversation; he had no idea what the other three were thinking. He noticed the beers were low and thought about another round. Thinking about anything else was just too dark.

"The weird thing is, if Tiffany hadn't been iced, you never would have known what was going on in those apartments," said Hamish.

"I mean, we were investigating," said Mulally. "But you're right – we didn't have a high priority on it. And Dory would still be scamming money…a little here, a little there. She had been doing it for years."

"Right," said Kevin. "She was processing fake purchases, doubling up supply orders and pocketing the difference. The pattern was clear once internal audit looked it over – she had been very tidy in keeping all the amounts below the threshold that would trigger suspicion. Of course, she said she was planning to pay it all back. That's what they all say."

"Kevin has become quite an expert in forensic accounting," Mulally said proudly.

"Show Smitty that real estate listing," Hamish prodded.

Kevin tapped at his phone to pull up the images of Dory's oceanfront house and passed it to Smitty.

"Zoom in on the boat," said Hamish, leaning over.

"Holy shit. I am so in the wrong business," said Smitty, passing the phone to Hamish.

"Looks just like my place," Hamish smiled. He pulled a toothpick from his wallet and placed it between his teeth, then passed the phone to Mulally, who squinted over his glasses at it.

"It's strange, the amount of money we could

document doesn't even come close to explaining that boat and the waterfront views," Kevin mused, still bugged by the unanswered questions littering the perimeter of the investigation.

"Maybe she was lucky in her gambling at first," Smitty said. "Anyway, looks like a great place to run prostitutes going forward." Hamish snickered and Smitty smiled, vindicated.

"She was in way over her head. Those low-level goons don't mess around on debts. That was hilarious that she thought you guys would scare them off." Hamish harked back to Dory's explanation of why she had called in the missing artwork.

Kevin and Mulally exchanged a quick glance; they were both glad the case was over, and they no longer needed to deal with these blowhards every day. Hamish really was a drama queen; general counsel Chu had been right about that.

"Well, cheers to all of us. Today's bad guys are locked up and out of our hair," Mulally raised his cup and they all toasted. "Peace and tranquility are restored to our humble campus."

Hamish added, "You did good police work; you solved the crime and caught the bad guys. Now you can go back to whatever it is you usually do – combat grade inflation or whatsis."

Mulally couldn't resist the chance to make his favorite speech. He took a deep pull on his beer and slapped the empty cup down on the table. "People always think the university is some kind of ivory tower Disney movie, where absent-minded professors think big thoughts and unicorns spurt rainbows out their assholes. Like there's no need for law enforcement here. Bullshit. Human beings are sinners no matter where they work. I have literally seen it all."

"Touched a nerve, huh?" asked Hamish.

"Prostitutes, thieves, murder. Jesus. Stolen

paintings," said Mulally.

Kevin resisted the urge to say *etchings* and noticed that his beer was also empty.

Hamish asked, "What about that asshole, Fernside?"

"What about that beef you've got going with the mayor?" Mulally responded.

Kevin groaned, got up and walked into the bar to get four more beers. The warmth and darkness inside were a relief. As he gestured to the barkeep, Hamish appeared at his left elbow and said to the man, "Make that three beers. I need to motor."

Turning to Kevin, he said, "I mean it - that was good police work, man. You ever think about joining the city force?"

"Every day for the first five years I worked here," Kevin replied.

"And how long have you worked here?

"Going on eight years now."

"What changed?"

"Oh, the usual. I got a couple promotions; saw some interesting cases. Like this one. I've been taking graduate classes at night – there's a tuition benefit. I'm working on a master's degree." He didn't say in what.

"Maybe you're getting too comfortable." Hamish suggested.

"Maybe…" Kevin was noncommittal.

"Well, it's been a pleasure. Your old man would've been proud. If you're looking for a change, give me a call. I'll put in a good word for you."

The barkeep handed the dripping cups across the mahogany. As Kevin reached for his wallet, Hamish said, "I need to run…but I've got these. Stay in touch."

Kevin took the three beers back to the patio. When Smitty saw that Hamish had left, he stood up to go as well. Standing there, he drained his fresh beer in a single, long swig. Setting the empty cup on the table, he said a loud, "Ahh…" and stifled a burp while rubbing his broad midsection with both hands.

Charming, thought Kevin. *What a knucklehead.*

"Gentlemen, it's been a pleasure," Smitty said.

"A real team effort," said Mulally, reaching out for a handshake. Smitty's departure left just Kevin and Mulally at the table. Kevin pulled out his cigarettes, offering the pack to Mulally who nodded and took one. They lit up, enjoying the quiet gesture.

"Well, good thing you've got the paperwork all finished," Mulally ventured.

Kevin grimaced.

"Yeah, that's what I thought." There was a twinkle in Mulally's eye as he lifted his plastic cup and bumped it against Kevin's. "Case closed; good work." They both took a satisfying pull on their beers.

"Did he offer you a job?" Mulally asked.

Kevin smiled. "I like it where I am. One murder is enough for me."

Mulally nodded. "Good man."

Kevin asked, "Nice redirect on that question about Fensbridge."

Mulally, still looking at his beer, snickered. "Yeah, it's none of his goddamn business. Fensbridge is an asshole, but for now, he's our asshole. This time, he wasn't the guy we were looking for."

Kevin's mouth formed a tight smile as he nodded philosophically into his beer, but his forehead stayed creased. Fensbridge was a loose end, a pebble in his shoe. He stole the art, but since it never technically left university property, it didn't register as theft. He compromised a young woman both sexually and professionally. But with Amanda keeping mum, there were no grounds for an ethics case. He'd misused university assets by breaking into 12C for sex. And he'd used his considerable influence for cronyism, enabling years of embezzlement. Basically, he'd acted like a crime boss with total impunity. Kevin's only consolation was that, since Fensbridge was sure to continue his rapacious ways, they would live to fight another day.

For now, Fensbridge and Amanda Herring weren't mentioned in the official report. They weren't relevant to the main story; the professor's crappy shenanigans seemed to be just a footnote to the case – and everyone knows there are no footnotes in police reports. The report laid out just the necessary facts, not every dead end that Kevin had pursued.

Mulally disturbed Kevin's reverie. "So, what did we learn?" It was a standard campstat question. "We'll need to talk it through next Wednesday morning." Kevin nodded, and his mind ranged far beyond the single case, pulling threads of what he'd learned from Sheila and Marie-Claude, from his latest visits to his mother at Glenhurst, from Larry and Reinaldo, from Jason and figure drawing. He had surprised himself with his immediate, clear response to Hamish's question about a job in the city. For the first time, he had had the chance to see that life up close, and now he knew for sure it wasn't for him.

Kevin felt Mulally watching, patiently allowing him to gather his thoughts. He took another sip of beer, feeling it slide coolly down his throat. He thought of his father's maxims.

"One step at a time. We were right not to rush to judgment – we learned more that way. We also found allies in some unexpected places by following the leads and treating everyone right."

Mulally nodded. "Most people are good. It's important to stay focused on that, and it can be tough in our line of work. It's one of the things I love about working at the U – being surrounded by smart, accomplished people who are pushing the state of knowledge forward. It's inspiring." It was rare for Mulally to wax philosophical, and his words, along with the beer, made Kevin want to express something deeper.

"There's a lot of wisdom here – even right in CAMPO. I appreciate that, and I'm still learning from you every day." Kevin swallowed a lump in his throat and dragged on his cigarette to mask his emotion.

Mulally nodded. "Thank you for saying that. I've enjoyed watching you 'grow up' here. Your family would be proud, especially your dad."

Kevin, at that moment, felt hopeful about his future. He stubbed out his cigarette and looked over at his boss. "We should write a book," he said. "Nobody would ever believe this stuff."

Debra Iles

ACKNOWLEDGMENTS

Many thanks to Amanda Gillette and Kay Ireland for editorial guidance, to Teresa Turvey for proofreading and copy editing, and to pwaperpro on Fiverr for cover art and design.

Made in the USA
Monee, IL
13 November 2023

46461375R00129